W9-BEH-375

J.G BALLARD was born in 1930 in Shanghai, China, where his father was a businessman. Following the attack on Pearl Harbor, Ballard and his family were placed in a civilian prison camp. They returned to England in 1946. After two years at Cambridge, where he read medicine, Ballard worked as a copywriter and Covent Garden porter before going to Canada with the RAF. He started writing short stories in the late 1950s, while working on a scientific journal. His first major novel, *The Drowned World*, was published in 1962. His acclaimed novels include *The Crystal World*, *The Atrocity Exhibition*, *Crash* (filmed by David Cronenberg), *High-Rise*, *The Unlimited Dream Company*, *The Kindness of Women* (the sequel to *Empire of the Sun*), *Cocaine Nights*, *Super-Cannes*, *Millennium People* and, most recently, *Kingdom Come*.

Visit www.AuthorTracker.co.uk for exclusive information on your favourite HarperCollins authors.

From the reviews of *The Atrocity Exhibition*:

'A powerful book ... phrase and image are constantly disturbing and stimulating. The central figure is a doctor moving through an underworld of psychosis. Reality and fantasy glide into each other. His chosen guides are the token figures of late-twentieth-century violence'     *Sunday Telegraph*

'*The Atrocity Exhibition* plays variations on the theme of human cruelty through the surrealistic glimpses of car crashes, images of decay and destruction, and public figures imagined in odd sexual attitudes'     *Sunday Times*

'A doctor suffering from a nervous breakdown is obsessed by images of violence: the assassination of President Kennedy, car crash victims, the death of Marilyn Monroe. Escaping from hospital, he rationalizes these fantasies by restaging events of violence in a way that he considers will give them new meanings - a disturbing book'     *Irish Times*

By the same author

# J.G. BALLARD

# *The Atrocity Exhibition*

Donation from the library of
Jose Pedro Segundo
1922 - 2022
Please pass freely to others readers so
that everyone can enjoy this book!

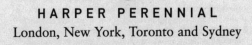

**HARPER PERENNIAL**
London, New York, Toronto and Sydney

Harper Perennial
An imprint of HarperCollins*Publishers*
77-85 Fulham Palace Road
Hammersmith, London W6 8JB

www.harperperennial.co.uk

This edition published by Harper Perennial 2006
9

A revised, expanded, annotated illustrated edition was previously published in
paperback by Flamingo 2001 (as a Flamingo Modern Classic, reprinted 5 times)
and in large format in Great Britain by Flamingo in 1993

A revised, expanded, annotated, illustrated edition was first published in the USA
by Re/Search Publications 1990

Copyright © J.G. Ballard 1990

The original edition was first published in Great Britain by Jonathan Cape Ltd
1970, and first published in paperback by Panther Books in 1972

Copyright © J.G. Ballard 1969

PS Section copyright © HarperCollins*Publishers* 2006, except 'The Smile' by
J. G. Ballard © J. G. Ballard 1976 and 'An Investigative Spirit', 'A Writing Life'
and 'Top Ten Books' © Travis Elborough 2006

PS™ is a trademark of HarperCollins*Publishers* Ltd

J.G. Ballard asserts the moral right to be identified as the author of this work.

This novel is entirely a work of fiction. The names, characters and incidents
portrayed in it are the work of the author's imagination. Any resemblance to
actual persons, living or dead, events or localities is entirely coincidental.

A catalogue record for this book is available from the British Library

ISBN-13:  978-0-00-711686-7
ISBN-10:  0-00-711686-1

Typeset in New Baskerville and Gill Sans by
Rowland Phototypesetting Ltd, Bury St Edmunds, Suffolk

Printed and bound in Great Britain by Clays Ltd, St Ives plc

All rights reserved. No part of this publication may be
reproduced, stored in a retrieval system, or transmitted,
in any form or by any means, electronic, mechanical,
photocopying, recording or otherwise, without the
prior permission of the publishers.

This book is sold subject to the condition that it shall not,
by way of trade or otherwise, be lent, re-sold, hired out or
otherwise circulated without the publisher's prior consent
in any form of binding or cover other than that in which it
is published and without a similar condition including this
condition being imposed on the subsequent purchaser.

# CONTENTS

# AUTHOR'S NOTE

Most of the film stars and political figures who appear in *The Atrocity Exhibition* are still with us, in memory if not in person – John F. Kennedy, Ronald Reagan, Marilyn Monroe and Elizabeth Taylor. Together they helped to form the culture of celebrity that played such a large role in the 1960s, when I wrote *The Atrocity Exhibition*.

Other figures, though crucially important to the decades that followed, have begun to sink below the horizon. How many of us remember Abraham Zapruder, who filmed the Kennedy assassination in Dallas? Or Sirhan Sirhan, who murdered Robert Kennedy? At the end of each chapter I have provided a few notes that identify these lesser characters and set out the general background to the book.

Readers who find themselves daunted by the unfamiliar narrative structure of *The Atrocity Exhibition* – far simpler than it seems at first glance – might try a different approach. Rather than start at the beginning of each chapter, as in a conventional novel, simply turn the pages until a paragraph catches your eye. If the ideas or images seem interesting, scan the nearby paragraphs for anything that resonates in an intriguing way. Fairly soon, I hope, the fog will clear, and the underlying narrative will reveal itself. In effect, you will be reading the book in the way it was written.

J.G. Ballard, 2001

# PREFACE BY WILLIAM BURROUGHS

*The Atrocity Exhibition* is a profound and disquieting book. The nonsexual roots of sexuality are explored with a surgeon's precision. An auto-crash can be more sexually stimulating than a pornographic picture. (Surveys indicate that wet dreams in many cases have no overt sexual content, whereas dreams with an overt sexual content in many cases do not result in orgasm.) The book opens: 'A disquieting feature of this annual exhibition ... was the marked preoccupation of the paintings with the theme of world cataclysm, as if these long-incarcerated patients had sensed some seismic upheaval within the minds of their doctors and nurses.'

The line between inner and outer landscapes is breaking down. Earthquakes can result from seismic upheavals within the human mind. The whole random universe of the industrial age is breaking down into cryptic fragments: 'In a waste lot of wrecked cars he found the burnt body of the white Pontiac, the nasal prepuce of LBJ, crashed helicopters, Eichmann in drag, a dead child ...' The human body becomes landscape: 'A hundred-foot-long panel that seemed to represent a section of sand dune ... Looking at it more closely Doctor Nathan realized that it was an immensely magnified portion of the skin over the iliac crest ...' This magnification of image to the point where it becomes unrecognizable is a keynote of *The*

*Atrocity Exhibition.* This is what Bob Rauschenberg is doing in art – literally *blowing up* the image. Since people are made of image, this is literally an explosive book. The human image explodes into rocks and stones and trees: 'The porous rock towers of Tenerife exposed the first spinal landscape ... clinker-like rock towers suspended above the silent swamp. In the mirror of this swamp there are no reflections. Time makes no concessions.'

Sexual arousal results from the repetition and impact of image: 'Each afternoon in the deserted cinema: the latent sexual content of automobile crashes ... James Dean, Jayne Mansfield, Albert Camus ... Many volunteers became convinced that the fatalities were still living and later used one or the other of the crash victims as a private focus of arousal during intercourse with the domestic partner.'

James Dean kept a hangman's noose dangling in his living room and put it around his neck to pose for news pictures. A painter named Milton, who painted a sexy picture entitled 'The Death of James Dean,' subsequently committed suicide. This book stirs sexual depths untouched by the hardest-core illustrated porn. 'What will follow is the psychopathology of sex relationships so lunar and abstract that people will become mere extensions of the geometries of situations. This will allow the exploration without any trace of guilt of every aspect of sexual psychopathology.'

Immensely magnified portion of James Dean subsequently committed suicide. Conception content relates to sexual depths of the hardest minds. Eichmann in drag in a waste lot of wrecked porous rock.

CHAPTER ONE

## THE ATROCITY EXHIBITION

**Apocalypse.** A disquieting feature of this annual exhibition – to which the patients themselves were not invited – was the marked preoccupation of the paintings with the theme of world cataclysm, as if these long-incarcerated patients had sensed some seismic upheaval within the minds of their doctors and nurses. As Catherine Austin walked around the converted gymnasium these bizarre images, with their fusion of Eniwetok and Luna Park, Freud and Elizabeth Taylor, reminded her of the slides of exposed spinal levels in Travis's office. They hung on the enamelled walls like the codes of insoluble dreams, the keys to a nightmare in which she had begun to play a more willing and calculated role. Primly she buttoned her white coat as Dr Nathan approached, holding his gold-tipped cigarette to one nostril. 'Ah, Dr Austin ... What do you think of them? I see there's War in Hell.'

**Notes Towards a Mental Breakdown.** The noise from the cine-films of induced psychoses rose from the lecture theatre below Travis's office. Keeping his back to the window behind his desk, he assembled the terminal documents he had collected with so much effort during the previous months: (1) Spectro-heliogram of the sun; (2) Front elevation of balcony units, Hilton Hotel, London; (3) Transverse section through a pre-Cambrian trilobite;

1

(4) 'Chronograms,' by E. J. Marey; (5) Photograph taken at noon, August 7th, 1945, of the sand-sea, Qattara Depression, Egypt; (6) Reproduction of Max Ernst's 'Garden Airplane Traps'; (7) Fusing sequences for 'Little Boy' and 'Fat Boy', Hiroshima and Nagasaki A-Bombs. When he had finished Travis turned to the window. As usual, the white Pontiac had found a place in the crowded parking lot directly below him. The two occupants watched him through the tinted windshield.

**Internal Landscapes.** Controlling the tremor in his left hand, Travis studied the thin-shouldered man sitting opposite him. Through the transom the light from the empty corridor shone into the darkened office. His face was partly hidden by the peak of his flying cap, but Travis recognized the bruised features of the bomber pilot whose photographs, torn from the pages of *Newsweek* and *Paris-Match*, had been strewn around the bedroom of the shabby hotel in Earls Court. His eyes stared at Travis, their focus sustained only by a continuous effort. For some reason the planes of his face failed to intersect, as if their true resolution took place in some as yet invisible dimension, or required elements other than those provided by his own character and musculature. Why had he come to the hospital, seeking out Travis among the thirty physicians? Travis had tried to speak to him, but the tall man made no reply, standing by the instrument cabinet like a tattered mannequin. His immature but at the same time aged face seemed as rigid as a plaster mask. For months Travis had seen his solitary figure, shoulders hunched inside the flying jacket, in more and more newsreels, as an extra in war films, and then as a patient in an elegant ophthalmic film on nystagmus – the series of giant geometric models, like sections of abstract landscapes, had made him uneasily aware that their long-delayed confrontation would soon take place.

**The Weapons Range.** Travis stopped the car at the end of the lane. In the sunlight he could see the remains of the outer perimeter fence, and beyond this a rusting quonset and the iron-stained roofs of the bunkers. He crossed the ditch and walked towards the fence, within five minutes found an opening. A disused runway moved through the grass. Partly concealed by the sunlight, the camouflage patterns across the complex of towers and bunkers four hundred yards away revealed half-familiar contours – the model of a face, a posture, a neural interval. A unique event would take place here. Without thinking, Travis murmured, 'Elizabeth Taylor.' Abruptly there was a blare of sound above the trees.

**Dissociation: Who Laughed at Nagasaki?** Travis ran across the broken concrete to the perimeter fence. The helicopter plunged towards him, engine roaring through the trees, its fans churning up a storm of leaves and paper. Twenty yards from the fence Travis stumbled among the coils of barbed wire. The helicopter was banking sharply, the pilot crouched over the controls. As Travis ran forward the shadows of the diving machine flickered around him like cryptic ideograms. Then the craft pulled away and flew off across the bunkers. When Travis reached the car, holding the torn knee of his trousers, he saw the young woman in the white dress walking down the lane. Her disfigured face looked back at him with indulgent eyes. Travis started to call to her, but stopped himself. Exhausted, he vomited across the roof of the car.

**Serial Deaths.** During this period, as he sat in the rear seat of the Pontiac, Travis was preoccupied by his separation from the normal tokens of life he had accepted for so long. His wife, the patients at the hospital (resistance agents in the 'world war' he hoped to launch), his undecided affair with Catherine Austin – these became as fragmentary as the faces of Elizabeth Taylor and Sigmund Freud on the advertising billboards, as unreal as the war the film companies had restarted in Vietnam. As he moved deeper into his own psychosis, whose onset he had recognized during his year at the hospital, he welcomed this journey into a familiar land, zones of twilight. *At dawn, after driving all night, they reached the suburbs of Hell. The pale flares from the petrochemical plants illuminated the wet cobbles. No one would meet them there.* His two companions, the bomber pilot at the wheel in the faded flying suit and the beautiful young woman with radiation burns, never spoke to him. Now and then the young woman would look at him with a faint smile on her deformed mouth. Deliberately, Travis made no response, hesitant to commit himself into her hands. Who were they, these strange twins – couriers from his own unconscious? For hours they drove through the endless suburbs of the city. The billboards multiplied around them, walling the streets with giant replicas of napalm bombings in Vietnam, the serial deaths of Elizabeth Taylor and Marilyn Monroe terraced in the landscapes of Dien Bien Phu and the Mekong Delta.

**Casualties Union.** At the young woman's suggestion, Travis joined the C.U., and with a group of thirty housewives practised the simulation of wounds. Later they would tour with Red Cross demonstration teams. Massive cerebral damage and abdominal bleeding in automobile accidents could be imitated within half an hour, aided by the application of suitable coloured resins. Convincing radiation burns required careful preparation, and might involve some three to four hours of makeup. Death, by contrast, was a matter of lying prone. Later, in the apartment they had taken overlooking the zoo, Travis washed the wounds from his hands and face. This curious pantomime, overlaid by the summer evening stench of the animals, seemed performed solely to pacify his two companions. In the bathroom mirror he could see the tall figure of the pilot, his slim face with its lost eyes hidden below the peaked cap, and the young woman in the white dress watching him from the lounge. Her intelligent face, like that of a student, occasionally showed a nervous reflex of hostility. Already Travis found it difficult not to think of her continuously. When would she speak to him? Perhaps, like himself, she realized that his instructions would come from other levels?

**Pirate Radio.** There were a number of secret transmissions to which Travis listened: (1) medullary: images of dunes and craters, pools of ash that contained the terraced faces of Freud, Eatherly, and Garbo; (2) thoracic: the rusting shells of U-boats beached in the cove at Tsingtao, near the ruined German forts where the Chinese guides smeared bloody handprints on the caisson walls; (3) sacral: V.J.-Day, the bodies of Japanese troops in the paddy fields at night. The next day, as he walked back to Shanghai, the peasants were planting rice among the swaying legs. Memories of others than himself, together these messages moved to some kind of focus. The dead face of the bomber pilot hovered by the door, the projection of World War III's unknown soldier. His presence exhausted Travis.

**Marey's Chronograms.** Dr Nathan passed the illustration across his desk to Margaret Travis. 'Marey's Chronograms are multiple-exposure photographs in which the element of time is visible – the walking human figure, for example, is represented as a series of dune-like lumps.' Dr Nathan accepted a cigarette from Catherine Austin, who had sauntered forward from the incubator at the rear of the office. Ignoring her quizzical eye, he continued, 'Your husband's brilliant feat was to reverse the process. Using a series of photographs of the most commonplace objects – this office, let us say, a panorama of New York skyscrapers, the naked body of a woman, the face of a catatonic patient – he treated them as if they already were chronograms and *extracted* the element of time.' Dr Nathan lit his cigarette with care. 'The results were extraordinary. A very different world was revealed. The familiar surroundings of our lives, even our smallest gestures, were seen to have totally altered meanings. As for the reclining figure of a film star, or this hospital . . .'

**'Was my husband a doctor, or a patient?'** Dr Nathan nodded sagely, glancing over his fingertips at Catherine Austin. What had Travis seen in those time-filled eyes? 'Mrs Travis, I'm not sure the question is valid any longer. These matters involve a relativity of a very different kind. What we are concerned with now are the implications – in particular, the complex of ideas and events represented by World War III. Not the political and military possibility, but the inner identity of such a notion. For us, perhaps, World War III is now little more than a sinister pop art display, but for your husband it has become an expression of the failure of his psyche to accept the fact of its own consciousness, and of his revolt against the present continuum of time and space. Dr Austin may disagree, but it seems to me that his intention is to start World War III, though not, of course, in the usual sense of the term. The blitzkriegs will be fought out on the spinal battlefields, in terms of the postures we assume, of our traumas mimetized in the angle of a wall or balcony.'

**Zoom Lens.** Dr Nathan stopped. Reluctantly, his eyes turned across the room to the portrait camera mounted on its tripod by the consulting couch. How could he explain to this sensitive and elusive woman that her own body, with its endlessly familiar geometry, its landscapes of touch and feeling, was their only defence against her husband's all-too-plain intentions? Above all, how could he invite her to pose for what she would no doubt regard as a set of obscene photographs?

**The Skin Area.** After their meeting, at the exhibition of war wounds at the Royal Society of Medicine's conference hall, Travis and Catherine Austin returned to the apartment overlooking the zoo. In the lift Travis avoided her hands as she tried to embrace him. He led her into the bedroom. Mouth pursed, she watched as he showed her the set of Enneper's models. 'What are they?' She touched the interlocking cubes and cones, mathematical models of pseudo-space. 'Fusing sequences, Catherine – for a doomsday weapon.' In the postures they assumed, in the contours of thigh and thorax, Travis explored the geometry and volumetric time of the bedroom, and later of the curvilinear roof of the Festival Hall, the jutting balconies of the London Hilton, and lastly of the abandoned weapons range. Here the circular target areas became identified in Travis's mind with the concealed breasts of the young woman with radiation burns. Searching for her, he and Catherine Austin drove around the darkening countryside, lost among the labyrinth of billboards. The faces of Sigmund Freud and Jeanne Moreau presided over their last bitter hours.

**Neoplasm.** Later, escaping from Catherine Austin, and from the forbidding figure of the bomber pilot, who now watched him from the roof of the lion house, Travis took refuge in a small suburban house among the reservoirs of Staines and Shepperton. He sat in the empty sitting-room overlooking the shabby garden. From the white bungalow beyond the clapboard fence his middle-aged neighbour dying of cancer watched him through the long afternoons. Her handsome face, veiled by the laced curtains, resembled that of a skull. All day she would pace around the small bedroom. At the end of the second month, when the doctor's visits became more frequent, she undressed by the window, exposing her emaciated body through the veiled curtains. Each day, as he watched from the cubular room, he saw different aspects of her eroded body, the black breasts reminding him of the eyes of the bomber pilot, the abdominal scars like the radiation burns of the young woman. After her death he followed the funeral cars among the reservoirs in the white Pontiac.

**The Lost Symmetry of the Blastosphere.** 'This reluctance to accept the fact of his own consciousness,' Dr Nathan wrote, 'may reflect certain positional difficulties in the immediate context of time and space. The right-angle spiral of a stairwell may remind him of similar biases within the chemistry of the biological kingdom. This can be carried to remarkable lengths – for example, the jutting

8

balconies of the Hilton Hotel have become identified with the lost gill-slits of the dying film actress, Elizabeth Taylor. Much of Travis's thought concerns what he terms "the lost symmetry of the blastosphere" – the primitive precursor of the embryo that is the last structure to preserve perfect symmetry in all planes. It occurred to Travis that our own bodies may conceal the rudiments of a symmetry not only about the vertical axis but also the horizontal. One recalls Goethe's notion that the skull is formed of modified vertebrae – similarly, the bones of the pelvis may constitute the remains of a lost sacral skull. The resemblance between histologies of lung and kidney has long been noted. Other correspondences of respiratory and urino-genital function come to mind, enshrined both in popular mythology (the supposed equivalence in size of nose and penis) and psychoanalytic symbolism (the "eyes" are a common code for the testicles). In conclusion, it seems that Travis's extreme sensitivity to the volumes and geometry of the world around him, and their immediate translation into psychological terms, may reflect a belated attempt to return to a symmetrical world, one that will recapture the perfect symmetry of the blastosphere, and the acceptance of the "Mythology of the Amniotic Return". In his mind World War III represents the final self-destruction and imbalance of an asymmetric world. The human organism is an atrocity exhibition at which he is an unwilling spectator . . .'

**Eurydice in a Used Car Lot.** Margaret Travis paused in the empty foyer of the cinema, looking at the photographs in the display frames. In the dim light beyond the curtains she saw the dark-suited figure of Captain Webster, the muffled velvet veiling his handsome eyes. The last few weeks had been a nightmare – Webster with his long-range camera and obscene questions. He seemed to take a certain sardonic pleasure in compiling this one-man Kinsey Report on her ... positions, planes, where and when Travis placed his hands on her body – why didn't he ask Catherine Austin? As for wanting to magnify the photographs and paste them up on enormous billboards, ostensibly to save her from Travis ... She glanced at the stills in the display frames, of this elegant and poetic film in which Cocteau had brought together all the myths of his own journey of return. On an impulse, to annoy Webster, she stepped through the side exit and walked past a small yard of cars with numbered windshields. Perhaps she would make her descent here. Eurydice in a used car lot?

**The Concentration City.** In the night air they passed the shells of concrete towers, blockhouses half buried in rubble, giant conduits filled with tyres, overhead causeways crossing broken roads. Travis followed the bomber pilot and the young woman along the faded gravel. They walked across the foundation of a guard-house into the weapons range. The concrete aisles stretched into the darkness across the airfield. *In the suburbs of Hell Travis walked in the flaring light of the petrochemical plants. The ruins of abandoned cinemas stood at the street corners, faded billboards facing them across the empty streets. In a waste lot of wrecked cars he found the burnt body of the white Pontiac. He wandered through the deserted suburbs.* The crashed bombers lay under the trees, grass growing through their wings. The bomber pilot helped the young woman into one of the cockpits. Travis began to mark out a circle on the concrete target area.

**How Garbo Died.** 'The film is a unique document,' Webster explained, as he led Catherine Austin into the basement cinema. 'At first sight it seems to be a strange newsreel about the latest tableau sculptures – there are a series of plaster casts of film stars and politicians in bizarre poses – how they were made we can't find out, they seem to have been cast from the living models, LBJ and Mrs Johnson, Burton and the Taylor actress, there's even one of Garbo dying. We were called in when the film was found.' He signalled to the projectionist. 'One of the casts is of Margaret Travis – I won't describe it, but you'll see why we're worried. Incidentally, a touring version of Kienholz's "Dodge 38" was seen travelling at speed on a motorway yesterday, a wrecked white car with the plastic dummies of a World War III pilot and a girl with facial burns making love among a refuse of bubblegum war cards and oral contraceptive wallets.'

**War-Zone D.** On his way across the car park Dr Nathan stopped and shielded his eyes from the sun. During the past week a series of enormous signs had been built along the roads surrounding the hospital, almost walling it in from the rest of the world. A group of workmen on a scaffolding truck were pasting up the last of the displays, a hundred-foot-long panel that appeared to represent a section of a sand-dune. Looking at it more closely, Dr Nathan realized that in fact it was an immensely magnified portion of the skin over the iliac crest. Glancing at the billboards, Dr Nathan recognized other magnified fragments: a segment of lower lip, a right nostril, a portion of female perineum. Only an anatomist would have identified these fragments, each represented as a formal geometric pattern. At least five hundred of the signs would

11

be needed to contain the whole of this gargantuan woman, terraced here into a quantified sand-sea. A helicopter soared overhead, its pilot supervising the work of the men on the track. Its down-draught ripped away some of the paper panels. They floated across the road, an eddying smile plastered against the radiator grille of a parked car.

**The Atrocity Exhibition.** Entering the exhibition, Travis sees the atrocities of Vietnam and the Congo mimetized in the 'alternate' death of Elizabeth Taylor; he tends the dying film star, eroticizing her punctured bronchus in the over-ventilated verandas of the London Hilton; he dreams of Max Ernst, superior of the birds; 'Europe after the Rain'; the human race – Caliban asleep across a mirror smeared with vomit.

**The Danger Area.** Webster ran through the dim light after Margaret Travis. He caught her by the entrance to the main camera bunker, where the cheekbones of an enormous face had been painted in faded Technicolor across the rust-stained concrete. 'For God's sake –' She looked down at his strong wrist against her breast, then wrenched herself away. 'Mrs Travis! Why do you think we've taken all these photographs?' Webster held the torn lapel of his suit, then pointed to a tableau figure in the uniform of a Chinese infantryman standing at the end of the conduit. 'The place is crawling with the things – you'll never find him.' As he spoke a searchlight in the centre of the airfield lit up the target areas, outlining the rigid figures of the mannequins.

**The Enormous Face.** Dr Nathan limped along the drainage culvert, peering at the huge figure of a dark-haired woman painted on the sloping walls of the blockhouse. The magnification was enormous. The wall on his right, the size of a tennis court, contained little more than the right eye and cheekbone. He recognized the woman from the billboards he had seen near the hospital – the screen actress, Elizabeth Taylor. Yet these designs were more than enormous replicas. They were equations that embodied the relationship between the identity of the film actress and the audiences who were distant reflections of her. The planes of their lives interlocked at oblique angles, fragments of personal myths fusing with the commercial cosmologies. The presiding deity of their lives the film actress provided a set of operating formulae for their passage through consciousness. Yet Margaret Travis's role was ambiguous. In some way Travis would attempt to relate his wife's body, with its familiar geometry, to that of the film actress, quantifying their identities to the point where they became fused with the elements of time and landscape. Dr Nathan crossed an exposed causeway to the next bunker. He leaned against the dark décolleté. When the searchlight flared between the blockhouses he put on his shoe. 'No . . .' He was hobbling towards the airfield when the explosion lit up the evening air.

**The Exploding Madonna.** For Travis, the ascension of his wife's body above the target area, exploding madonna of the weapons range, was a celebration of the intervals through which he perceived the surrounding continuum of time and space. Here she became one with the madonnas of the billboards and the ophthalmic films, the Venus of the magazine cuttings whose postures celebrated his own search through the suburbs of Hell.

13

**Departure.** The next morning, Travis wandered along the gunnery aisles. On the bunkers the painted figure of the screen actress mediated all time and space to him through her body. As he searched among the tyres and coils of barbed wire he saw the helicopter rising into the sky, the bomber pilot at the controls. It made a leftward turn and flew off towards the horizon. Half an hour later the young woman drove away in the white Pontiac. Travis watched them leave without regret. When they had gone the corpses of Dr Nathan, Webster, and Catherine Austin formed a small tableau by the bunkers.

**A Terminal Posture.** Lying on the worn concrete of the gunnery aisles, he assumed the postures of the film actress, assuaging his past dreams and anxieties in the dune-like fragments of her body.

*Apocalypse.*
'Eniwetok and Luna Park' may seem a strange pairing, the H-bomb test site in the Marshall Islands with the Paris fun-fair loved by the surrealists. But the endless newsreel clips of nuclear explosions that we saw on TV in the 1960s (a powerful incitement to the psychotic imagination, sanctioning *everything*) did have a carnival air, a media phenomenon which Stanley Kubrick caught perfectly at the end of *Dr Strangelove*. I imagine my mental patients conflating Freud and Liz Taylor in their Warhol-like efforts, unerringly homing in on the first signs of their doctor's nervous breakdown. *The Atrocity Exhibition*'s original dedication should have been 'To the Insane'. I owe them everything.

*Notes Towards a Mental Breakdown.*
The many lists in *The Atrocity Exhibition* were produced by free association, which accounts for the repetition but, I hope, makes more sense of them.

'Garden Airplane Traps.' 'Voracious gardens in turn devoured by a vegetation that springs from the debris of trapped airplanes.' Max Ernst, *Informal Life*. The nightmare of a grounded pilot.

Why a white Pontiac? A British pop-star of the 1960s, Dickie Valentine, drove his daughter in a white Pontiac to the same school that my own children attended near the film studios at Shepperton. The car had a powerful iconic presence, emerging from all those American movies into the tranquil TV suburbs. Soon after, Valentine died in a car accident. By chance a telescoped Pontiac starred in my 1969 exhibition of crashed cars at the New Arts Laboratory in London.

*The Weapons Range.*
Weapons ranges have a special magic, all that destructive technology concentrated on the production of nothing, the closest we can get to certain obsessional states of mind. Even more strange are the bunkers of the Nazi Atlantic Wall, most of which are still standing, and are far larger than one expects. Space-age cathedrals, they threaten the surrounding landscape like lines of Teutonic knights, and are examples of cryptic architecture, where form no longer reveals function. They seem to contain the codes of some mysterious mental process. At Utah Beach, the most deserted stretch of the Normandy coast, they stare out over the washed sand, older than the planet. On visits with my agent and his wife, I used to photograph them compulsively.

*Serial Deaths.*
'The war the film companies had restarted in Vietnam.' Written in 1966, this was a prophetic leap in the dark. To date no Vietnam movie has been shot on the original battlegrounds, but I'm confident it will happen, and might even get out of control. Spielberg returned to Shanghai for *Empire of the Sun*, an eerie sensation for me – even more so were the scenes shot near Shepperton, using extras recruited from among my neighbours, many of whom have part-time jobs at the studios. I can almost believe that I came to Shepperton thirty years ago knowing

unconsciously that one day I would write a novel about my wartime experiences in Shanghai, and that it might well be filmed in these studios. Deep assignments run through all our lives; there are no coincidences.

*Casualties Union.*

The so-called Casualties Union existed in London in the 1960s, probably inspired by the nuclear disarmament movement. Putting on the cosmetic wounds was a messy business, and a recruitment leaflet reassured volunteers: 'Death is simply a matter of lying prone.'

*Pirate Radio.*

Tsingtao, on the north China coast near Peking, was a German naval base during World War I, and later became a popular beach resort where I spent the summers in the 1930s. As a seven-year-old I was deeply impressed by the huge blockhouses and the maze of concrete tunnels where the tourist guides pointed to the bloody handprints of (they claimed) wounded German gunners driven mad by the British naval bombardment. For some reason these were far more moving than the dead Chinese soldiers in the battle-grounds around Shanghai which I visited with my parents, though they were sad enough.

*Marey's Chronograms.*

'An individual is a four-dimensional object of greatly elongated form; in ordinary language we say that he has considerable extension in time and insignificant extension in space.' Eddington, *Space, Time and Gravitation.*

*The Lost Symmetry of the Blastosphere.*

Elizabeth Taylor was staying at the Hilton during the shooting of Cleopatra, when she contracted pneumonia and was given a trache-otomy. The Hilton's balconies remind Travis of the actress's lost gill-slits (which we all develop embryonically as we briefly recapitulate our biological past).

*Eurydice in a Used Car Lot.*
'Where and when Travis placed his hands on her body.' The poet Paul Eluard, describing his wife Gala, who later left him to marry Dali, said: 'Her body is the shape of my hands.'

*How Garbo Died.*
The sculptor George Segal has made a number of plaster casts of prominent art patrons, mostly New York bankers and their wives. Frozen in time, these middle-aged men and women have a remarkable poignancy, figures from some future Pompeii.

*The Enormous Face.*
Elizabeth Taylor, the last of the old-style Hollywood actresses, has retained her hold on the popular imagination in the two decades since this piece was written, a quality she shares (no thanks to myself) with almost all the public figures in this book – Marilyn Monroe, Reagan, Jackie Kennedy among others. A unique collision of private and public fantasy took place in the 1960s, and may have to wait some years to be repeated, if ever. The public dream of Hollywood for the first time merged with the private imagination of the hyper-stimulated 60s TV viewer. People have sometimes asked me to do a follow-up to *The Atrocity Exhibition*, but our perception of the famous has changed – I can't imagine writing about Meryl Streep or Princess Di, and Margaret Thatcher's undoubted mystery seems to reflect design faults in her own self-constructed persona. One can mechanically spin sexual fantasies around all three, but the imagination soon flags. Unlike Taylor, they radiate no light.

A kind of banalisation of celebrity has occurred: we are now offered an instant, ready-to-mix fame as nutritious as packet soup. Warhol's screen-prints show the process at work. His portraits of Marilyn Monroe and Jackie Kennedy drain the tragedy from the lives of these desperate women, while his day-glo palette returns them to the innocent world of the child's colouring book.

17

## CHAPTER TWO

# THE UNIVERSITY OF DEATH

**The Conceptual Death.** By now these seminars had become a daily inquisition into Talbot's growing distress and uncertainty. A disturbing aspect was the conscious complicity of the class in his long anticipated breakdown. Dr Nathan paused in the doorway of the lecture theatre, debating whether to end this unique but unsavoury experiment. The students waited as Talbot stared at the photographs of himself arranged in sequence on the blackboard, his attention distracted by the elegant but severe figure of Catherine Austin watching from the empty seats beside the film projector. The simulated newsreels of auto-crashes and Vietnam atrocities (an apt commentary on her own destructive sexuality) illustrated the scenario of World War III on which the students were ostensibly engaged. However, as Dr Nathan realized, its real focus lay elsewhere. An unexpected figure now dominated the climax of the scenario. Using the identity of their own lecturer, the students had devised the first conceptual death.

**Auto-erotic.** As he rested in Catherine Austin's bedroom, Talbot listened to the helicopters flying along the motorway from the airport. Symbols in a machine apocalypse, they seeded the cores of unknown memories in the furniture of the apartment, the gestures of unspoken affections.

He lowered his eyes from the window. Catherine Austin sat on the bed beside him. Her naked body was held forward like a bizarre exhibit, its anatomy a junction of sterile cleft and flaccid mons. He placed his palm against the mud-coloured areola of her left nipple. The concrete landscape of underpass and overpass mediated a more real presence, the geometry of a neural interval, the identity latent within his own musculature.

**Obscene Mannequin.** 'Shall I lie down with you?' Ignoring her question, Talbot studied her broad hips, with their now empty contours of touch and feeling. Already she had the texture of a rubber mannequin fitted with explicit vents, an obscene masturbatory appliance. As he stood up he saw the diaphragm in her handbag, useless *cache-sexe*. He listened to the helicopters. They seemed to alight on an invisible landing zone in the margins of his mind. On the garage roof stood the sculpture he had laboriously built during the past month; antennae of metal aerials holding glass faces to the sun, the slides of diseased spinal levels he had taken from the laboratory. All night he watched the sky, listening to the time-music of the quasars.

**Left Orbit and Temple.** Below the window a thickset young man, wearing the black military overcoat affected by the students, was loading a large display billboard into a truck outside the Neurology department, a photo reproduction of Talbot's left orbit and temple. He stared up at the sculpture on the roof. His sallow, bearded face had pursued Talbot for the past weeks during the conception of the scenario. It was at Koester's instigation that the class were now devising the optimum death of World War III's first casualty, a wound profile more and more clearly revealed as Talbot's. A marked physical hostility existed between them, a compound of sexual rivalry over Catherine Austin and homo-erotic jealousy.

**A Sophisticated Entertainment.** Dr Nathan gazed at the display photographs of terminal syphilitics in the cinema foyer. Already members of the public were leaving. Despite the scandal that would ensue he had deliberately authorized this 'Festival of Atrocity Films,' which Talbot had suggested as one of his last coherent acts. Behind their display frames the images of Nader and JFK, napalm and air crash victims revealed the considerable ingenuity of the film makers. Yet the results were disappointing; whatever Talbot had hoped for had clearly not materialized. The violence was little more than a sophisticated entertainment. One day he would carry out a Marxist analysis of this lumpen intelligentsia. More properly, the programme should be called a festival of home movies. He lit a gold-tipped cigarette, noticing that a photograph of Talbot had been cleverly montaged over a reproduction of Dali's 'Hypercubic Christ.' Even the film festival had been devised as part of the scenario's calculated psycho-drama.

**A Shabby Voyeur.** As she parked the car, Karen Novotny could see the silver bowls of the three radio telescopes above the trees. The tall man in the shabby flying jacket walked towards the perimeter fence, bars of sunlight crossing his face. Why had she followed him here? She had picked him up in the empty hotel cinema after the conference on space medicine, then taken him back to her apartment. All week he had been watching the telescopes with the same fixity of expression, an optical rigor like that of a disappointed voyeur. Who was he? – some fugitive from time and space, clearly moving now into his own landscape. His room was filled with grotesque magazine photographs: the obsessive geometry of over-passes, like fragments of her own body; X-rays of unborn children; a series of genital deformations; a hundred close-ups of hands. She stepped from the car, the coil hanging in her womb like a steel foetus, a stillborn star. She smoothed her white linen skirt as Talbot ran back from the fence, ripping the cassette from his camera. Between them had sprung up a relationship of intense sexuality.

**The Image Maze.** Talbot followed the helicopter pilot across the rain-washed concrete. For the first time, as he wandered along the embankment, one of the aircraft had landed. The slim figure of the pilot left no reflections in the silver pools. The exhibition hall was deserted. Beyond a tableau sculpture of a Saigon street execution stood a maze constructed from photographic billboards. The pilot stepped through a doorway cut into an image of Talbot's face. He looked up at the photograph of himself, snapped with a lapel camera during his last seminar. Over the exhausted eyes presided the invisible hierarchies of the quasars. Reading the maze, Talbot made his way among the corridors. Details of his hands and mouth signposted its significant junctions.

**Spinal Levels.** 'Sixties iconography: the nasal prepuce of LBJ, crashed helicopters, the pudenda of Ralph Nader, Eichmann in drag, the climax of a New York happening: a dead child. In the patio at the centre of the maze a young woman in a flowered white dress sat behind a desk covered with catalogues. Her blanched skin exposed the hollow planes of her face. Like the pilot, Talbot recognized her as a student at his seminar. Her nervous smile revealed the wound that disfigured the inside of her mouth.

**Towards the D.M.Z.** Later, as he sat in the cabin of the helicopter, Talbot looked down at the motorway below them. The speeding cars wound through the cloverleaves. The concrete causeways formed an immense cipher, the templates of an unseen posture. The young woman in the white dress sat beside him. Her breasts and shoulders recapitulated the forgotten contours of Karen Novotny's body, the motion-sculpture of the highways. Afraid to smile at him, she stared at his hands as if they held some invisible weapon. The flowering tissue of her mouth reminded him of the porous esplanades of Ernst's 'Silence,' the pumice-like beaches of a dead sea. His committal into the authority of these two couriers had at last freed him from his memories of Koester and Catherine Austin. The erosion of that waking landscape continued. Meanwhile the quasars burned dimly from the dark peaks of the universe, sections of his brain reborn in the island galaxies.

**Mimetized Disasters.** The helicopter banked abruptly, pulled round in a gesture of impatience by the pilot. They plunged towards the underpass, the huge fans of the Sikorsky sliding through the air like the wings of a crippled archangel. A multiple collision had occurred in the approach to the underpass. *After the police had left they walked for an hour among the cars, staring through the steam at the bodies propped against the fractured windshields. Here he would find his alternate death, the mimetized disasters of Vietnam and the Congo recapitulated in the contours of these broken fenders* *and radiator assemblies.* As they circled overhead the shells of the vehicles lay in the dusk like the crushed wings of an aerial armada.

**No U-Turn.** 'Above all, the notion of conceptual auto-disaster has preoccupied Talbot during the final stages of his breakdown,' Dr Nathan wrote. 'But even more disturbing is Talbot's deliberate self-involvement in the narrative of the scenario. Far from the students making an exhibition of an overwrought instructor, transforming him into a kind of ur-Christ of the communications landscape, Talbot has in fact exploited them. This has altered the entire direction of the scenario, turning it from an exercise on the theme of "the end of the world" into a psycho-drama of increasingly tragic perspectives.'

**The Persistence of Memory.** An empty beach with its fused sand. Here clock time is no longer valid. Even the embryo, symbol of secret growth and possibility, is drained and limp. These images are the residues of a remembered moment of time. For Talbot the most disturbing elements are the rectilinear sections of the beach and sea. The displacement of these two images through time, and their marriage with his own continuum, has warped them into the rigid and unyielding structures of his own consciousness. Later, walking along the overpass, he realized that the rectilinear forms of his conscious reality were warped elements from some placid and harmonious future.

**Arrival at the Zone.** They sat in the unfading sunlight on the sloping concrete. The abandoned motorway ran off into the haze, silver firs growing through its sections. Shivering in the cold air, Talbot looked out over the landscape of broken overpasses and crushed underpasses. The pilot walked down the slope to a rusting grader surrounded by tyres and fuel drums. Beyond it a quonset tilted into a pool of mud. Talbot waited for the young woman to speak to him, but she stared at her hands, lips clenched against her teeth. Against the drab concrete the white fabric of her dress shone with an almost luminescent intensity. How long had they sat there?

**The Plaza.** Later, when his two couriers had moved to the ridge of the embankment, Talbot began to explore the terrain. Covered by the same even light, the landscape of derelict roadways spread to the horizon. On the ridge the pilot squatted under the tail of the helicopter, the young woman behind him. Their impassive, unlit faces seemed an extension of the landscape. Talbot followed the concrete beach. Here and there sections of the banking had fallen, revealing the steel buttresses below. An orchard of miniature fruit trees grew from the sutures between the concrete slabs. Three hundred yards from the helicopter he entered a sunken plaza where two convergent highways moved below an underpass. The shells of long-abandoned automobiles lay below the arches. Talbot brought the young woman and guided her down the embankment. For several hours they waited on the concrete slope. The geometry of the plaza exercised a unique fascination upon Talbot's mind.

**The Annunciation.** Partly veiled by the afternoon clouds, the enormous image of a woman's hands moved across the sky. Talbot stood up, for a moment losing his balance on the sloping concrete. Raised as if to form an arch over an invisible child, the hands passed through the air above the plaza. They hung in the sunlight like immense doves. Talbot climbed the slope, following this spectre along the embankment. He had witnessed the annunciation of a unique event. Looking down at the plaza, he murmured without thinking, 'Ralph Nader.'

**The Geometry of Her Face.** In the perspectives of the plaza, the junctions of the underpass and embankment, Talbot at last recognized a modulus that could be multiplied into the landscape of his consciousness. The descending triangle of the plaza was repeated in the facial geometry of the young woman. The diagram of her bones formed a key to his own postures and musculature, and to the scenario that had preoccupied him at the Institute. He began to prepare for departure. The pilot and the young woman now deferred to him. The fans of the helicopter turned in the dark air, casting elongated ciphers on the dying concrete.

**Transliterated Pudenda.** Dr Nathan showed his pass to the guard at the gatehouse. As they drove towards the testing area he was aware of Catherine Austin peering through the windshield, her sexuality keening now that Talbot was within range. Nathan glanced down at her broad thighs, calculating the jut and rake of her pubis. 'Talbot's belief – and this is confirmed by the logic of the scenario – is that automobile crashes play very different roles from the ones we assign them. Apart from its manifest function, redefining the elements of space and time in terms of our most potent consumer durable, the car crash may be perceived unconsciously as a fertilizing rather than a destructive event – a liberation of sexual energy – mediating the sexuality of those who have died with an intensity impossible in any other form: James Dean and Miss Mansfield, Camus and the late President. In the eucharist of the simulated auto-disaster we see the transliterated pudenda of Ralph Nader, our nearest image of the blood and body of Christ.' They stopped by the test course. A group of engineers watched a crushed Lincoln dragged away through the morning air. The hairless plastic mannequin of a woman sat propped on the grass, injury sites marked on her legs and thorax.

**Journeys to an Interior.** Waiting in Karen Novotny's apartment, Talbot made certain transits: (1) Spinal: 'The Eye of Silence' – these porous rock towers, with the luminosity of exposed organs, contained an immense planetary silence. Moving across the iodine water of these corroded lagoons, Talbot followed the solitary nymph through the causeways of rock, the palaces of his own flesh and bone. (2) Media: montage landscapes of war – webbing heaped in pits beside the Shanghai–Nanking railway; bargirls' cabins built out of tyres and fuel drums; dead Japanese stacked like firewood in L.C.T.s off Woosung pier. (3) Contour: the unique parameters of Karen's body – beckoning vents of mouth and vulva, the soft hypogeum of the anus. (4) Astral: segments of his posture mimetized in the processions of space. These transits contained an image of the geometry assembling itself in the musculature of the young woman, in their postures during intercourse, in the angles between the walls of the apartment.

**Stochastic Analysis.** Karen Novotny paused over the wet stockings in the handbasin. As his fingers touched her armpits she stared into the sculpture garden between the apartment blocks. The sallow-faced young man in the fascist overcoat who had followed her all week was sitting on the bench beside the Paolozzi. His paranoid eyes, with their fusion of passion and duplicity, had watched her like a rapist's across the café tables. Talbot's bruised hands were lifting her breasts, as if weighing their heavy curvatures against some more plausible alternative. The landscape of highways obsessed him, the rear mouldings of automobiles. All day he had been building his bizarre antenna on the roof of the apartment block, staring into the sky as if trying to force a corridor to the sun. Searching in his suitcase, she found clippings of his face taken from as yet unpublished news stories in *Oggi* and *Newsweek*. In the evening, while she bathed, waiting for him to enter the bathroom as she powdered her body, he crouched over the blueprints spread between the sofas in the lounge, calculating a stochastic analysis of the Pentagon car park.

**Crash Magazine.** Catherine Austin moved through the exhibits towards the dark-skinned young man in the black coat. He leaned against one of the cars, his face covered by the rainbows reflected from a frosted windshield. Who was Koester: a student in Talbot's class; Judas in this scenario; a rabbi serving a sinister novitiate? Why had he organized this exhibition of crashed cars? The truncated vehicles, with their ruptured radiator grilles, were arranged in lines down the showroom floor. His warped sexuality, of which she had been aware since his arrival at the first semester, had something of the same quality as these maimed vehicles. He had even produced a magazine devoted solely to car accidents: *Crash!* The dismembered bodies of Jayne Mansfield, Camus and Dean presided over its pages, epiphanies of violence and desire.

**A Cosmetic Problem.** The star of the show was JFK, victim of the first conceptual car crash. A damaged Lincoln had been given the place of honour, plastic models of the late President and his wife in the rear seat. An elaborate attempt had been made to represent cosmetically the expressed brain tissue of the President. As she touched the white acrylic smears across the trunk Koester swung himself aggressively out of the driver's seat. While he lit her cigarette she leaned against the fender of a white Pontiac, their thighs almost touching. Koester took her arm with a nervous gesture. 'Ah, Dr Austin . . .' The flow of small talk modulated their sexual encounter. '. . . surely Christ's crucifixion could be regarded as the first traffic accident – certainly if we accept Jarry's happy piece of anti-clericalism . . .'

**The Sixty-Minute Zoom.** As they moved from apartment to apartment along the motorway, Karen Novotny was conscious of the continuing dissociation of the events around her. Talbot followed her about the apartment, drawing chalk outlines on the floor around her chair, around the cups and utensils on the breakfast table as she drank her coffee, and lastly around herself: (1) sitting, in the posture of Rodin's 'Thinker', on the edge of the bidet, (2) watching from the balcony as she waited for Koester to find them again, (3) making love to Talbot on the bed. He worked silently at the chalk outlines, now and then rearranging her limbs. The noise of the helicopters had become incessant. One morning she awoke in complete silence to find that Talbot had gone.

**A Question of Definition.** The multiplying outlines covered the walls and floors, a frieze of priapic dances –

crash victims, a crucified man, children in intercourse. The outline of a helicopter covered the cinder surface of the tennis court like the profile of an archangel. She returned after a fruitless search among the cafés to find the furniture removed from the apartment. Koester and his student gang were photographing the chalk outlines. Her own name had been written into the silhouette of herself in the bath. ' "Novotny, masturbating," ' she read out aloud. 'Are you writing me into your scenario, Mr Koester?' she asked with an attempt at irony. His irritated eyes compared her figure with the outline in the bath. '*We* know where he is, Miss Novotny.' She stared at the outline of her breasts on the black tiles of the shower stall, Talbot's hands traced around them. Hands multiplied around the rooms, soundlessly clapping, a welcoming host.

**The Unidentified Female Orifice.** These leg stances pre-occupied Talbot – Karen Novotny (1) stepping from the driving seat of the Pontiac, median surface of thighs exposed, (2) squatting on the bathroom floor, knees laterally displaced, fingers searching for the diaphragm lip, (3) in the *a tergo* posture, thighs pressing against Talbot, (4) collision: crushed right tibia against the instrument console, left patella impacted by the handbrake.

**The Optimum Wound Profile.** 'One must bear in mind that roll-over followed by a head-on collision produces complex occupant movements and injuries from unknown sources,' Dr Nathan explained to Captain Webster. He held up the montage photograph he had found in Koester's cubicle, the figure of a man with itemized wound areas. 'However, here we have a wholly uncharacteristic emphasis on palm, ankle, and abdominal injuries. Even allowing for the excessive crushing movements in a severe impact it is difficult to reconstruct the likely accident mode. In this case, taken from Koester's scenario of Talbot's death, the injuries seem to have been sustained in an optimized auto-fatality, conceived by the driver as some kind of bizarre crucifixion. He would be mounted in the crash vehicle in an obscene position as if taking part in some grotesque act of intercourse – Christ crucified on the sodomized body of his own mother.'

**The Impact Zone.** At dusk Talbot drove around the deserted circuit of the research laboratory test track. Grass grew waist high through the untended concrete, wheel-less cars rusted in the undergrowth along the verge. Overhead the helicopter moved across the trees, its fans churning up a storm of leaves and cigarette cartons. Talbot steered the car among the broken tyres and oil drums. Beside him the young woman leaned against his shoulder, her grey eyes surveying Talbot with an almost minatory calm. He turned on to a concrete track between the trees. The collision course ran forwards through the dim light, crushed cars shackled to steel gondolas above a catapult. Plastic mannequins spilled through the burst doors and panels. As they walked along the catapult rails Talbot was aware of the young woman pacing out the triangle of approach roads. Her face contained the geometry of the plaza. He worked until dawn, towing the wrecks into the semblance of a motorcade.

**Talbot: False Deaths.** (1) The flesh impact: Karen Novotny's beckoning figure in the shower stall, open thighs and exposed pubis – traffic fatalities screamed in this soft collision. (2) The overpass below the apartment: the angles between the concrete buttresses contained for Talbot an immense anguish. (3) A crushed fender: in its broken geometry Talbot saw the dismembered body of Karen Novotny, the alternate death of Ralph Nader.

**Unusual Poses.** 'You'll see why we're worried, Captain.' Dr Nathan beckoned Webster towards the photographs pinned to the walls of Talbot's office. 'We can regard them in all cases as "poses". They show (1) the left orbit and zygomatic arch of President Kennedy magnified from Zapruder frame 230, (2) X-ray plates of the hands of Lee Harvey Oswald, (3) a sequence of corridor angles at the Broadmoor Hospital for the Criminally Insane, (4) Miss Karen Novotny, an intimate of Talbot's, in a series of unusual amatory positions. In fact, it is hard to tell whether the positions are those of Miss Novotny in intercourse or as an auto-crash fatality – to a large extent the difference is now meaningless.' Captain Webster studied the exhibits. He fingered the shaving scar on his heavy jaw, envying Talbot the franchises of this young woman's body. 'And together they make up a portrait of this American safety fellow – Nader?'

**'In Death, Yes.'** Nathan nodded sagely over his cigarette smoke. 'In *death*, yes. That is, an alternate or "false" death. These images of angles and postures constitute not so much a private gallery as a conceptual equation, a fusing device by which Talbot hopes to bring his scenario to a climax. The danger of an assassination attempt seems evident, one hypotenuse in this geometry of a murder. As to the figure of Nader – one must remember that Talbot is here distinguishing between the manifest content of reality and its latent content. Nader's true role is clearly very different from his apparent one, to be deciphered in terms of the postures we assume, our anxieties mimetized in the junction between wall and ceiling. In the post-Warhol era a single gesture such as uncrossing one's legs will have more significance than all the pages in *War and Peace*. In twentieth-century terms the crucifixion, for example, would be re-enacted as a conceptual auto-disaster.'

**Idiosyncrasies and Sin-crazed Idioms.** As she leaned against the concrete parapet of the camera tower, Catherine Austin could feel Koester's hands moving around her shoulder straps. His rigid face was held six inches from her own, his mouth like the pecking orifice of some unpleasant machine. The planes of his cheekbones and temples intersected with the slabs of rain-washed cement, together forming a strange sexual modulus. A car moved along the perimeter of the test area. During the night the students had built an elaborate tableau on the impact site fifty feet below, a multi-vehicle auto-crash. A dozen wrecked cars lay on their sides, broken fenders on the grass verges. Plastic mannequins had been embedded in the interlocked windshields and radiator grilles, wound areas marked on their broken bodies. Koester had named them: Jackie, Ralph, Abraham. Perhaps he saw the tableau as a rape? His hand hesitated on her left breast. He was watching the Novotny girl walking along the concrete aisle. She laughed, disengaging herself from Koester. Where were her own wound areas?

**Speed Trials.** Talbot opened the door of the Lincoln and took up his position in agent Greer's seat. Behind him the helicopter pilot and the young woman sat in the rear of the limousine. For the first time the young woman had begun to smile at Talbot, a soundless rictus of the mouth, deliberately exposing her wound as if showing him that her shyness had gone. Ignoring her now, Talbot looked out through the dawn light at the converging concrete aisles. Soon the climax of the scenario would come, JFK would die again, his young wife raped by this conjunction of time and space. The enigmatic figure of Nader presided over the collision, its myths born from the cross-overs of auto-crashes and genitalia. He looked up from the wheel as the flares illuminated the impact zone. When the car surged forward he realized that the two passengers had gone.

**The Acceleration Couch.** Half zipping his trousers, Koester lay back against the torn upholstery, one hand still resting on the plump thigh of the sleeping young woman. The debris-filled compartment had not been the most comfortable site. This zombie-like creature had strayed across the concrete runways like a fugitive from her own dreams, forever talking about Talbot as if unconsciously inviting Koester to betray him. Why was she wearing the Jackie Kennedy wig? He sat up, trying to open the rusty door. The students had christened the wreck 'Dodge 38', furnishing the rear seat with empty beer bottles and contraceptive wallets. Abruptly the car jolted forward, throwing him across the young woman. As she woke, pulling at her skirt, the sky whirled past the frosted windows. The clanking cable between the rails propelled them on a collision course with a speeding limousine below the camera tower.

**Celebration.** For Talbot the explosive collision of the two cars was a celebration of the unity of their soft geometries, the unique creation of the pudenda of Ralph Nader. The dismembered bodies of Karen Novotny and himself moved across the morning landscape, re-created in a hundred crashing cars, in the perspectives of a thousand concrete embankments, in the sexual postures of a million lovers.

**Interlocked Bodies.** Holding the bruise under his left nipple, Dr Nathan ran after Webster towards the burning wrecks. The cars lay together at the centre of the collision corridor, the last steam and smoke lifting from their cabins. Webster stepped over the armless body of Karen Novotny hanging face-down from the rear window. The burning fuel had traced a delicate lacework of expressed tissue across her naked thighs. Webster pulled open the rear door of the Lincoln. 'Where the hell is Talbot?' Holding his throat with one hand, Dr Nathan stared at the wig lying among the beer bottles.

**The Helicopters are Burning.** Talbot followed the young woman between the burning helicopters. Their fuselages formed bonfires across the dark fields. Her strong stride, with its itemized progress across the foam-smeared concrete, carried within its rhythm a calculated invitation to his own sexuality. Talbot stopped by the burning wreck of a Sikorsky. The body of Karen Novotny, with its landscapes of touch and feeling, clung like a wraith to his thighs and abdomen.

**Fractured Smile.** The hot sunlight lay across the suburban street. From the radio of the car sounded a fading harmonic. Karen Novotny's fractured smile spread across the windshield. Talbot looked up at his own face mediated from the billboard beside the car park. Overhead the glass curtain-walls of the apartment block presided over this first interval of neural calm.

*The Conceptual Death.*
Experiments often test the experimenter more than the subject. One remembers the old joke about the laboratory rat who said: 'I have that scientist trained – every time I press this lever he gives me a pellet of food.' For me, the most interesting aspect of the work of Masters and Johnson, collected in *Human Sexual Response*, was its effect on themselves. How were *their* sex lives influenced, what changes occurred in their sexual freedoms and fantasies? In conversation they seemed almost neutered by the experiments. I suspect that the copulating volunteers were really training the good doctors to lose all interest in sex, just as computerized diagnostic machines, where patients press buttons in reply to stock questions, are inadvertently training them to develop duodenal ulcers or varicose veins.

Talbot. Another face of the central character of *The Atrocity Exhibition*. The core identity is Traven, a name taken consciously from B. Traven, a writer I've always admired for his extreme reclusiveness – so completely at odds with the logic of our own age, when even the concept of privacy is constructed from publicly circulating materials. It is now almost impossible to be ourselves except on the world's terms.

*Obscene Mannequin.*
The time-music of the quasars. A huge volume of radio signals reaches this planet from space, crossing gigantic distances from the far side of the universe. It's hard to accept that these messages are meaningless, as they presumably are, no more than the outward sign of nuclear processes within the stars. Yet the hope remains that one day we will decode them, and find, not some intergalactic fax service, but a spontaneously generated choral music, a naive electro-magnetic archi-

tecture, the primitive syntax of a philosophical system, as meaningless but as reassuring as the pattern of waves on a beach.

Reassembling the furniture of his mind, Talbot has constructed a primitive antenna, and can now hear the night sky singing of time, the voice of the unseen powers of the cosmos.

### A Sophisticated Entertainment.

Has a festival of atrocity films ever been held? Every year at the Oscars ceremony, some might say. It seemed likely in the late 60s, but the new puritans of our day would greet such a suggestion with a shudder. A pity – given the unlimited opportunities which the media landscape now offers to the wayward imagination, I feel we should immerse ourselves in the most destructive element, ourselves, and swim. I take it that the final destination of the 20th century, and the best we can hope for in the circumstances, is the attainment of a moral and just psychopathology.

### The Image Maze.

After a dinner party in the 1970s I almost came to blows with a prominent New York poet (in fact, I tried playfully to run him down with my car, if such an act can be playful). He had derided my observation that cruel and violent images which elicit pity one day have by the next afternoon been stylised into media emblems. Yet the tragic photograph of the Saigon police chief shooting a Viet Cong suspect in the head was soon used by the London *Sunday Times* as a repeated logo keying its readers to Vietnam features in the paper. If I remember, the tilt of the dying man's head was slightly exaggerated, like a stylized coke bottle or tail-fin.

### Towards the D.M.Z.

Max Ernst's paintings run through *The Atrocity Exhibition*, in particular 'The Eye of Silence' and 'Europe After the Rain.' Their clinker-like rocks resemble skeletons from which all organic matter has been leached, all sense of time. Looking at these landscapes, it's impossible to imagine anything ever happening within them. The neural counterparts of these images must exist within our brains, though it's difficult to guess what purpose they serve.

*Mimetized Disasters.*
Most of the machines that surround our lives – airliners, refrigerators, cars and typewriters – have streamlined their way into our affections. Now and then, as in the case of the helicopter, with its unstable, insect-like obsessiveness, we can see clearly the deep hostility of the mineral world. We are lucky that the organic realm reached the foot of the evolutionary ladder before the inorganic.

*The Persistence of Memory.*
Dali's masterpiece, and one of the most powerful of all surrealist images.

*The Plaza.*
Dealey Plaza in Dallas, re-imagined in Talbot's eye as the end of the world.

*The Annunciation.*
Nader has only just survived into the 1990s, and it's difficult now to imagine his name leaping to anyone's lips, but at the time he sent a seismic tremor through the mind of the US consumer, challenging the authority of that greatest of all American icons, the automobile. Every car crash seemed a prayer to Ralph Nader.

*Stochastic Analysis.*
Believe it or not, some researcher did carry out a stochastic analysis of the Pentagon car park, translating the guesstimated flow-patterns of vehicles into a three-dimensional volume graph.

*Crash Magazine.*
This was written two years before my 1969 exhibition of crashed cars. Scouring the wreckers' yards around London, I was unable to find a

crashed Lincoln Continental, perhaps fortunately. As it was, the audience reaction to the telescoped Pontiac, Mini and Austin Cambridge verged on nervous hysteria, though had the cars been parked in the street outside the gallery no one would have given them a glance or devoted a moment's thought to the injured occupants. In a calculated test of the spectators, I hired a topless girl to interview the guests on closed-circuit TV. She had originally agreed to appear naked, but on seeing the cars informed me that she would only appear topless – an interesting logic was at work there. As the opening night party deteriorated into a drunken brawl she was almost raped in the back seat of the Pontiac, and later wrote a damning review of the show in the underground paper *Friendz*. The cars were exhibited without comment, but during the month-long show they were continually attacked by visitors to the gallery, who broke windows, tore off wing mirrors, splashed them with white paint. The overall reaction to the experiment convinced me to write *Crash*, in itself a considerable challenge to most notions of sanity.

I'm told that cars purporting to be the JFK Continental are often exhibited in the United States, and that a *white* Continental claiming to be the car in which Kennedy met his death was recently the centrepiece of a small museum on the causeway leading to Cocoa Beach, Florida.

*The Optimum Wound Profile.*

In February 1972, two weeks after completing *Crash*, I was involved in my only serious car accident. After a front wheel blowout my Ford Zephyr veered to the right, crossed the central reservation (I received a bill for the demolished sign, and was annoyed to see later that I had paid for a more advanced model, with flashing lights), and then rolled over and continued upside-down along the oncoming lane. Fortunately I was wearing a seat belt and no other vehicle was involved. An extreme case of nature imitating art. Curiously, before the accident and since, I have always been a careful and even slow driver, frequently egged on by impatient women-friends.

*Unusual Poses.*

Abraham Zapruder was a tourist in Dealey Plaza whose amateur cine-film captured the President's tragic death. The Warren Commission concluded that frame 210 recorded the first rifle shot, which wounded Kennedy in the neck, and that frame 313 recorded the fatal head wound. I forget the significance of frame 230.

The Warren Commission's Report is a remarkable document, especially if considered as a work of fiction (which many experts deem it largely to be). The chapters covering the exact geometric relationships between the cardboard boxes on the seventh floor of the Book Depository (a tour de force in the style of Robbe-Grillet), the bullet trajectories and speed of the Presidential limo, and the bizarre chapter titles – 'The Subsequent Bullet That Hit,' 'The Curtain Rod Story,' 'The Long and Bulky Package' – together suggest a type of obsessional fiction that links science and pornography. One shudders to think how the report's authors would have dealt with any sexual elements, particularly if they had involved Jacqueline Kennedy (perhaps *The Atrocity Exhibition* fills that gap), or how their successors might have coped with the assassination of Vice-President Quayle and his evangelist wife in a hotel suite – say in Miami, a good city in which to be assassinated, within sight of those lovely banyan trees in Coral Gables, ambling pelicans and the witty Arquitectonica building.

*Speed Trials.*

Special Agent William R. Greer of the Secret Service was the driver of the Presidential limousine. One can't help wondering how the events in Dealey Plaza affected him. Has his sense of space and time been altered? What role in his imagination is played by the desperate widow? The facilities exist for a complete neuro-psychiatric profile, though one will never be carried out. The results would be interesting, since we were all in a sense in the driver's seat on that day in Dallas.

## CHAPTER THREE

# THE ASSASSINATION WEAPON

**Thoracic Drop.** The spinal landscape, revealed at the level of T-12, is that of the porous rock towers of Tenerife, and of the native of the Canaries, Oscar Dominguez, who created the technique of decalcomania and so exposed the first spinal landscape. The clinker-like rock towers, suspended above the silent swamp, create an impression of profound anguish. The inhospitability of this mineral world, with its inorganic growths, is relieved only by the balloons flying in the clear sky. They are painted with names: Jackie, Lee Harvey, Malcolm. In the mirror of this swamp there are no reflections. Here, time makes no concessions.

**Autogeddon.** Waking: the concrete embankment of a motorway extension. Roadworks, cars drumming two hundred yards below. In the sunlight the seams between the sections are illuminated like the sutures of an exposed skull. A young woman stands ten feet away from him, watching with unsure eyes. The hyoid bone in her throat flutters as if discharging some subvocal rosary. She points to her car, parked off the verge beside a grader, and then beckons to him. *Kline, Coma, Xero.* He remembered the aloof, cerebral Kline and their long discussions on this terminal concrete beach. Under a different sun. This girl is not Coma. 'My car.' She speaks, the sounds as

41

dissociated as the recording in a doll. 'I can give you a lift. I saw you reach the island. It's like trying to cross the Styx.'

**Googolplex.** Dr Nathan studied the walls of the empty room. The mandalas, scored in the white plaster with a nail file, radiated like suns towards the window. He peered at the objects on the tray offered to him by the nurse. 'So, these are the treasures he has left us – an entry from Oswald's Historic Diary, a much-thumbed reproduction of Magritte's "Annunciation", and the mass numbers of the first twelve radioactive nuclides. What are we supposed to do with them?' Nurse Nagamatzu gazed at him with cool eyes. 'Permutate them, doctor?' Dr Nathan lit a cigarette, ignoring the explicit insolence. This elegant bitch, like all women she intruded her sexuality at the most inopportune moments. One day . . . He said, 'Perhaps. We might find Mrs Kennedy there. Or her husband. The Warren Commission has reopened its hearing, you know. Apparently it's not satisfied. Quite unprecedented.' Permutate them? The theoretical number of nucleotide patterns in DNA was a mere 10 to the power of 120,000. What number was vast enough to contain all the possibilities of those three objects?

**Jackie Kennedy, your eyelids deflagrate.** The serene face of the President's widow, painted on clapboard four hundred feet high, moves across the rooftops, disappearing into the haze on the outskirts of the city. There are hundreds of the signs, revealing Jackie in countless familiar postures. Next week there may be an SS officer, Beethoven, Christopher Columbus or Fidel Castro. The fragments of these signs litter the suburban streets for weeks afterwards. Bonfires of Jackie's face burn among the reservoirs of Staines and Shepperton. With luck he finds a job on one of the municipal disposal teams, warms his hands at a brazier of eyes. At night he sleeps beneath an unlit bonfire of breasts.

**Xero.** Of the three figures who were to accompany him, the strangest was Xero. For most of the time Kline and Coma would remain near him, sitting a few feet away on the embankment of the deserted motorway, following in another car when he drove to the radio-observatory, pausing behind him as he visited the atrocity exhibition. Coma was too shy, but now and then he would manage to talk to Kline, although he never remembered what they said to each other. By contrast, Xero was a figure of galvanic energy and uncertainty. As he moved across the abandoned landscape near the overpass, the perspectives of the air seemed to invert behind him. At times, when Xero approached the forlorn group sitting on the embankment, his shadows formed bizarre patterns on the concrete, transcripts of cryptic formulae and insoluble dreams. These ideograms, like the hieroglyphs of a race of blind seers, remained on the grey concrete after Xero had gone, the detritus of this terrifying psychic totem.

**Questions, always questions.** Karen Novotny watched him move around the apartment, dismantling the mirrors in the hall and bathroom. He stacked them on the table between the settees in the lounge. This strange man, and his obsessions with time, Jackie Kennedy, Oswald and Eniwetok. Who was he? Where had he come from? In the three days since she had found him on the motorway she had discovered only that he was a former H-bomber pilot,

43

for some reason carrying World War III in his head. 'What are you trying to build?' she asked. He assembled the mirrors into a box-like structure. He glanced up at her, face hidden by the peak of his Air Force cap. 'A trap.' She stood beside him as he knelt on the floor. 'For what? Time?' He placed a hand between her knees and gripped her right thigh, handhold of reality. 'For your womb, Karen. You've caught a star there.' But he was thinking of Coma, waiting with Kline in the espresso bar, while Xero roamed the street in his white Pontiac. In Coma's eyes runes glowed.

**The Impossible Room.** In the dim light he lay on the floor of the room. A perfect cube, its walls and ceiling were formed by what seemed to be a series of cinema screens. Projected on to them in close-up was the face of Nurse Nagamatsu, her mouth, three feet across, moving silently as she spoke in slow motion. Like a cloud, the giant head moved up the wall behind him, then passed across the ceiling and down the opposite corner. Later the inclined, pensive face of Dr Nathan appeared, rising from the floor until it filled three walls and the ceiling, a slow mouthing monster.

**Beach Fatigue.** After climbing the concrete incline, he reached the top of the embankment. The flat, endless terrain stretched away on all sides, a few oil derricks in the distance marking the horizon. Among the spilled sand and burst cement bags lay old tyres and beer bottles. Guam in 1947. He wandered away, straddling roadworks and irrigation ditches, towards a rusting quonset near the incline of the disused overpass. Here, in this terminal hut, he began to piece together some sort of existence. Inside the hut he found a set of psychological tests. Although he had no means of checking them, his answers seemed to establish an identity. He went off to forage, and came back to the hut with a collection of mud-stained documents and a Coke bottle.

**Pontiac Starchief.** Two hundred yards from the hut a wheel-less Pontiac sits in the sand. The presence of this car baffles him. Often he spends hours sitting in it, trying out the front and back seats. All sorts of rubbish is lying in the sand: a typewriter with half the keys missing (he picks out fragmentary sentences, sometimes these seem to mean something), a smashed neurosurgical unit (he pockets a handful of leucotomes, useful for self-defence). Then he cuts his foot on the Coke bottle, and spends several feverish days in the hut. Luckily he finds an incomplete isolation drill for trainee astronauts, half of an eighty-hour sequence.

**Coma: the million-year girl.** Coma's arrival coincides with his recovery from the bout of fever. At first she spends all her time writing poems on the damaged typewriter. Later, when not writing the poems, she wanders away to an old solar energy device and loses herself in the maze of mirrors. Shortly afterwards Kline appears, and sits at a chair and table in the sand twenty yards from the hut. Xero, meanwhile, is moving among the oil derricks half a mile away, assembling immense Cinemascope signs that carry the reclining images of Oswald, Jackie Kennedy and Malcolm X.

**Pre-uterine Claims.** 'The author,' Dr Nathan wrote, 'has found that the patient forms a distinctive type of object relation based on perpetual and irresistible desire to merge with the object in an undifferentiated mass. Although psychoanalysis cannot reach the primary archaic mechanism of "rapprochement" it can deal with the neurotic superstructure, guiding the patient towards the choice of stable and worthwhile objects. In the case under consideration the previous career of the patient as a military pilot should be noted, and the unconscious role of thermonuclear weapons in bringing about the total fusion and non-differentiation of all matter. What the patient is reacting against is, simply, the phenomenology of the universe, the specific and independent existence of separate objects and events, however trivial and inoffensive these may seem. A spoon, for example, offends him by the mere fact of its existence in time and space. More than this, one could say that the precise, if largely random, configuration of atoms in the universe at any given moment, one never again to be repeated, seems to him to be preposterous by virtue of its unique identity...' Dr Nathan lowered his pen and looked down into the recreation garden. Traven was standing in the sunlight, raising and lowering his arms and legs in a private calisthenic display, which he repeated several times (presumably an attempt to render time and events meaningless by replication?).

'But isn't Kennedy already dead?' Captain Webster studied the documents laid out on Dr Nathan's demonstration table. These were: (1) a spectroheliogram of the sun; (2) tarmac and take-off checks for the B-29 Superfortress Enola Gay; (3) electroencephalogram of Albert Einstein; (4) transverse section through a pre-Cambrian trilobite; (5) photograph taken at noon, August 7th, 1945, of the sand-sea, Qattara Depression; (6) Max Ernst's 'Garden Airplane Traps'. He turned to Dr Nathan. 'You say these constitute an assassination weapon?'

**'Not in the sense you mean.'** Dr Nathan covered the exhibits with a sheet. By chance the cabinets took up the contours of a corpse. 'Not in the sense you mean. This is an attempt to bring about the "false" death of the President – false in the sense of coexistent or alternate. The fact that an event has taken place is no proof of its valid occurrence.' Dr Nathan went over to the window. Obviously he would have to begin the search single-handedly. Where to begin? No doubt Nurse Nagamatzu could be used as bait. That vamp had once worked as a taxi-dancer in the world's largest nightclub in Osaka, appropriately named 'The Universe'.

**Unidentified Radio-source, Cassiopeia.** Karen Novotny waited as he reversed the car on to the farm track. Half a mile across the meadows she could see the steel bowls of the three radio telescopes in the sunlight. So the attempt was to be made here? There seemed to be nothing to kill except the sky. All week they had been chasing about, sitting for hours through the conference on neuropsychiatry, visiting art galleries, even flying in a rented Rapide across the reservoirs of Staines and Shepperton. Her eyes had ached from keeping a lookout. 'They're four hundred feet high,' he told her, 'the last thing you need is a pair of binoculars.' What had he been looking for – the radio telescopes or the giant madonnas he muttered about as he lay asleep beside her at night? 'Xero!' she heard him shout. With the agility of an acrobat he vaulted over the bonnet of the car, then set off at a run across the meadow. Carrying the black Jackie Kennedy wig as carefully as she could in both hands, she hurried after him. One of the telescopes was moving, its dish turning towards them.

**Madame Butterfly.** Holding the wound under her left breast, Nurse Nagamatzu stepped across Webster's body and leaned against the bogie of the telescope pylon. Eighty feet above her the steel bowl had stopped revolving, and the echoes of the gunshots reverberated among the lattice-work. Clearing her throat with an effort, she spat out the blood. The flecks of lung tissue speckled the bright ribbon of the rail. The bullet had broken two ribs, then collapsed her left lung and lodged itself below her scapula. As her eyes faded she caught a last glimpse of a white American car setting off across the tarmac apron beyond the control house, where the shells of the old bombers lay heaped together. The runways of the former airfield radiated from her in all directions. Dr Nathan was kneeling in the path of the car, intently building a sculpture of mirrors. She tried to pull the wig off her head, and then fell sideways across the rail.

**The Bride Stripped Bare by her Bachelors, Even.** Pausing outside the entrance to the tea terrace, Margaret Traven noticed the tall figure of Captain Webster watching her from the sculpture room. Duchamp's glass construction, on loan from the Museum of Modern Art, reminded her of the ambiguous role she might have to play. This was chess in which every move was a counter-gambit. How could she help her husband, that tormented man, pursued by furies more implacable than the Four Riders – the very facts of time and space? She gave a start as Webster took her elbow. He turned to face her, looking into her eyes. 'You need a drink. Let's sit down – I'll explain again why this is so important.'

**Venus Smiles.** The dead face of the President's widow looked up at him from the track. Confused by the Japanese cast of her features, with all their reminders of Nagasaki and Hiroshima, he stared at the bowl of the telescope. Twenty yards away Dr Nathan was watching him in the sunlight, the sculpture beside him reflecting a dozen fragments of his head and arms. Kline and Coma were moving away along the railway track.

**Einstein.** 'The notion that this great Swiss mathematician is a pornographer may strike you as something of a bad joke,' Dr Nathan remarked to Webster. 'However, you must understand that for Traven science is the ultimate pornography, analytic activity whose main aim is to isolate objects or events from their contexts in time and space. This obsession with the specific activity of quantified functions is what science shares with pornography. How different from Lautreamont, who brought together the sewing machine and the umbrella on the operating table, identifying the pudenda of the carpet with the woof of the cadaver.' Dr Nathan turned to Webster with a smile. 'One looks forward to the day when the *General Theory of Relativity* and the *Principia* will outsell the *Kama Sutra* in back-street bookshops.'

**Rune-filled Eyes.** Now, in this concluding phase, the presence of his watching trinity, Coma, Kline and Xero, became ever closer. All three were more preoccupied than he remembered them. Only Coma, with her rune-filled eyes, watched him with any sympathy. It was as if they sensed that something was missing. He remembered the documents he had found near the terminal hut.

**In a Technical Sense.** Webster's hand hesitated on Karen Novotny's zip. He listened to the last bars of the Mahler symphony playing from the radiogram extension in the warm bedroom. 'The bomber crashed on landing,' he explained. 'Four members of the crew were killed. He was alive when they got him out, but at one point in the operating theatre his heart and vital functions failed. In a technical sense he was dead for about two minutes. Now, all this time later, it looks as if something is missing, something that vanished during the short period of his death. Perhaps his soul, the capacity to achieve a state of grace. Nathan would call it the ability to accept the phenomenology of the universe, or the fact of your own consciousness. This is Traven's hell. You can see he's trying to build bridges between things – this Kennedy business, for example. He wants to kill Kennedy again, but in a way that makes sense.'

**The Water World.** Margaret Traven moved through the darkness along the causeways between the reservoirs. Half a mile away the edge of the embankment formed a raised horizon, enclosing this world of tanks, water and pumping gear with an almost claustrophobic silence. The varying levels of water in the tanks seemed to let an extra dimension into the damp air. A hundred yards away, across two parallel settling beds, she saw her husband walking rapidly along one of the white-painted catwalks. He disappeared down a stairway. What was he looking for? Was this watery world the site where he hoped to be reborn, in this fragmented womb with its dozens of amniotic levels?

**An Existential Yes.** They were moving away from him. After his return to the terminal hut he noticed that Kline, Coma and Xero no longer approached him. Their fading figures, a quarter of a mile from the hut, wandered to and fro, half-hidden from him by the hollows and earthworks. The Cinemascope billboards of Jackie, Oswald and Malcolm X were beginning to break up in the wind. One morning he woke to find that they had gone.

**The Terminal Zone.** He lay on the sand with the rusty bicycle wheel. Now and then he would cover some of the spokes with sand, neutralizing the radial geometry. The rim interested him. Hidden behind a dune, the hut no longer seemed a part of his world. The sky remained constant, the warm air touching the shreds of test papers sticking up from the sand. He continued to examine the wheel. Nothing happened.

*Thoracic Drop.*
Oscar Dominguez, a leading member of the surrealist group in Paris, invented the technique of crushing gouache between layers of paper. When separated they reveal eroded, rock-like forms that touch some deeply buried memory, perhaps at an early stage in the formation of the brain's visual centres, before the wiring is fully in place. Here I refer to Ernst's 'Eye of Silence'.

*Googolplex.*
Oswald's Historic Diary, which he began on October 16th, 1959, the day of his arrival in Moscow, is a remarkable document which shows

51

this inarticulate and barely literate man struggling to make sense of the largest issues of his day. Curiously, many prominent assassins have possessed distinctive literary styles, as if they had unconsciously rehearsed and rationalized their crimes on the verbal level long before committing them. Arthur Bremer, who critically wounded George Wallace, composed his own diary with great literary flair, while Manson has a unique apocalyptic style. 'Paycheck whore wears a dollar bill gown to the funeral of hope and love . . .' (*The Manson File*, Amok Press).

*Xero.*
These three figures, who are shadows projected from Traven's unconscious, had been in my mind since the end of the 1950s (see *Re/Search #8/9*, pages 38–40). They materialized in *The Atrocity Exhibition*, but then exited and never returned. I wait patiently for them to reappear.

*Beach Fatigue.*
Guam in 1947. The B-29s which bombed the airfield beside Lunghua Camp, near Shanghai, where I was interned during the Second World War, had reportedly flown from Guam. Pacific islands with their silent airstrips among the palm trees, Wake Island above all, have a potent magic for me. The runways that cross these little atolls, now mostly abandoned, seem to represent extreme states of nostalgia and possibility, doorways into another continuum. It was from the island of Tinian, in the Marianas, that the atom bombs were launched against Hiroshima and Nagasaki, which ended the war unexpectedly and almost certainly saved the lives of myself and my fellow internees in Shanghai, where the huge Japanese armies had intended to make a last stand against the expected American landings.

*'But isn't Kennedy already dead?'*
Kennedy's assassination presides over *The Atrocity Exhibition*, and in many ways the book is directly inspired by his death, and represents a desperate attempt to make sense of the tragedy, with its huge hidden

agenda. The mass media created the Kennedy we know, and his death represented a tectonic shift in the communications landscape, sending fissures deep into the popular psyche that have not yet closed.

*Unidentified Radio-source, Cassiopeia.*
Giant billboards can materialize in unexpected places. Twenty years after writing this, in December 1987, I arrived in Los Angeles for the first time, on my way to a movie. Driving down Santa Monica Boulevard I was struck by the total familiarity of the urban landscape, accurately presented in thousands of films and TV episodes. Then, to my amazement, I looked up at the first anomaly, a huge billboard that carried my own name, among others. Identical billboards reared over the city, even looking down on Sunset Boulevard, where another writer, Joe Gillis, had also found himself entangled in the Hollywood Dream. On a quiet Sunday I rented a Chevrolet in Beverly Hills (a car despised by the intelligent young women working for Warners and my New York publishers, who drove Hondas and BMWs) and drove around that mysterious city. The signs seemed to have escaped from my head, clambering over the rooftops like some monster in a 1950s s-f movie. The irony of being trapped inside the media maze I had described in *The Atrocity Exhibition* wasn't lost on me.

*Einstein.*
Pornography is under attack at present, thanks in part to the criminal excesses of kiddy porn and snuff movies, and to our newly puritan climate – the fin de siècle decadence that dominated the 1890s, and which we can expect to enliven the 1990s, may well take the form of an aggressive and over-the-top puritanism. A pity, I feel, since the sexual imagination is unlimited in scope and metaphoric power, and can never be successfully repressed. In many ways pornography is the most literary form of fiction – a verbal text with the smallest attachment to external reality, and with only its own resources to create a complex and exhilarating narrative. I commend Susan Sontag's brave 1969 essay

('The Pornographic Imagination'), though I would go much further in my claims. Pornography is a powerful catalyst for social change, and its periods of greatest availability have frequently coincided with times of greatest economic and scientific advance.

## CHAPTER FOUR

## YOU: COMA: MARILYN MONROE

**The Robing of the Bride.** At noon, when she woke, Tallis was sitting on the metal chair beside the bed, his shoulders pressed to the wall as if trying to place the greatest possible distance between himself and the sunlight waiting on the balcony like a trap. In the three days since their meeting at the beach planetarium he had done nothing but pace out the dimensions of the apartment, constructing some labyrinth from within. She sat up, aware of the absence of any sounds or movement in the apartment. He had brought with him an immense quiet. Through this glaciated silence the white walls of the apartment fixed arbitrary planes. She began to dress, aware of his eyes staring at her body.

**Fragmentation.** For Tallis, this period in the apartment was a time of increasing fragmentation. A pointless vacation had led him by some kind of negative logic to the small resort on the sand bar. In his faded cotton suit he had sat for hours at the tables of the closed cafés, but already his memories of the beach had faded. The adjacent apartment block screened the high wall of the dunes. The young woman slept for most of the day and the apartment was silent, the white volumes of the rooms extending themselves around him. Above all, the whiteness of the walls obsessed him.

**The 'Soft' Death of Marilyn Monroe.** Standing in front of him as she dressed, Karen Novotny's body seemed as smooth and annealed as those frozen planes. Yet a displacement of time would drain away the soft interstices, leaving walls like scraped clinkers. He remembered Ernst's 'Robing': Marilyn's pitted skin, breasts of carved pumice, volcanic thighs, a face of ash. The widowed bride of Vesuvius.

**Indefinite Divisibility.** At the beginning, when they met in the deserted planetarium among the dunes, he seized on Karen Novotny's presence. All day he had been wandering among the sand hills, trying to escape the apartment houses which rose in the distance above the dissolving crests. The opposing slopes, inclined at all angles to the sun like an immense Hindu yantra, were marked with the muffled ciphers left by his sliding feet. On the concrete terrace outside the planetarium the young woman in the white dress watched him approach with maternal eyes.

**Enneper's Surface.** Tallis was immediately struck by the unusual planes of her face, intersecting each other like the dunes around her. When she offered him a cigarette he involuntarily held her wrist, feeling the junction between the radius and ulna bones. He followed her across the dunes. The young woman was a geometric equation, the demonstration model of a landscape. Her breasts and buttocks illustrated Enneper's surface of negative constant curve, the differential coefficient of the pseudo-sphere.

**False Space and Time of the Apartment.** These planes found their rectilinear equivalent in the apartment. The right angles between the walls and ceiling were footholds in a valid system of time, unlike the suffocating dome of the planetarium, expressing its infinity of symmetrical boredom. He watched Karen Novotny walk through the rooms, relating the movements of her thighs and hips to the architectonics of floor and ceiling. This cool-limbed young woman was a modulus; by multiplying her into the space and time of the apartment he would obtain a valid unit of existence.

**Suite Mentale.** Conversely, Karen Novotny found in Tallis a visible expression of her own mood of abstraction, that growing entropy which had begun to occupy her life in the deserted beach resort since the season's end. She had been conscious for some days of an increasing sense of disembodiment, as if her limbs and musculature merely established the residential context of her body. She cooked for Tallis, and washed his suit. Over the ironing board she watched his tall figure interlocking with the dimensions and angles of the apartment. Later, the sexual act between them was a dual communion between themselves and the continuum of time and space which they occupied.

**The Dead Planetarium.** Under a bland, equinoctial sky, the morning light lay evenly over the white concrete outside the entrance to the planetarium. Near by, the hollow basins of cracked mud were inversions of the damaged dome of the planetarium, and of the eroded breasts of Marilyn Monroe. Almost hidden by the dunes, the distant apartment blocks showed no signs of activity. Tallis waited in the deserted café terrace beside the entrance, scraping with a burnt-out match at the gull droppings that had fallen through the tattered awning onto the green metal tables. He stood up when the helicopter appeared in the sky.

**A Silent Tableau.** Soundlessly the Sikorsky circled the dunes, its fans driving the fine sand down the slopes. It landed in a shallow basin fifty yards from the planetarium. Dr Nathan stepped from the aircraft, finding his feet uncertainly in the sand. The two men shook hands. After a pause, during which he scrutinized Tallis closely, the psychiatrist began to speak. His mouth worked silently, eyes fixed on Tallis. He stopped and then began again with an effort, lips and jaw moving in exaggerated spasms as if he were trying to extricate some gum-like residue from his teeth. After several intervals, when he had failed to make a single audible sound, he turned and went back to the helicopter. Without any noise it took off into the sky.

**Appearance of Coma.** She was waiting for him at the café terrace. As he took his seat she remarked, 'Do you lip-read? I won't ask what he was saying.' Tallis leaned back, hands in the pockets of his freshly pressed suit. 'He accepts now that I'm quite sane – at least, as far as the term goes; these days its limits seem to be narrowing. The problem is one of geometry, what these slopes and planes mean.' He glanced at Coma's broad-cheeked face. More and more she resembled the dead film star. What code would fit both this face and body and Karen Novotny's apartment?

**Dune Arabesque.** Later, walking across the dunes, he saw the figure of the dancer. Her muscular body, clad in white tights and sweater that made her almost invisible against

58

the sloping sand, moved like a wraith up and down the crests. She lived in the apartment facing Karen Novotny's, and would come out each day to practise among the dunes. Tallis sat down on the roof of a car buried in the sand. He watched her dance, a random cipher drawing its signature across the time-slopes of this dissolving yantra, a symbol in a transcendental geometry.

**Impressions of Africa.** A low shoreline; air glazed like amber; derricks and jetties above brown water; the silver geometry of a petrochemical complex, a Vorticist assemblage of cylinders and cubes superimposed upon the distant plateau of mountains; a single Horton sphere – enigmatic balloon tethered to the fused sand by its steel cradles; the unique clarity of the African light: fluted tablelands and jigsaw bastions; the limitless neural geometry of the landscape.

**The Persistence of the Beach.** The white flanks of the dunes reminded him of the endless promenades of Karen Novotny's body – diorama of flesh and hillock; the broad avenues of the thighs, piazzas of pelvis and abdomen, the closed arcades of the womb. This terracing of Karen's body in the landscape of the beach in some way diminished the identity of the young woman asleep in her apartment. He walked among the displaced contours of her pectoral girdle. What time could be read off the slopes and inclines of this inorganic musculature, the drifting planes of its face?

**The Assumption of the Sand-dune.** This Venus of the dunes, virgin of the time-slopes, rose above Tallis into the meridian sky. The porous sand, reminiscent of the eroded walls of the apartment, and of the dead film star with her breasts of carved pumice and thighs of ash, diffused along its crests into the wind.

**The Apartment: Real Space and Time.** The white rectilinear walls, Tallis realized, were aspects of that virgin of the sand-dunes whose assumption he had witnessed. The apartment was a box clock, a cubicular extrapolation of the facial planes of the yantra, the cheekbones of Marilyn Monroe. The annealed walls froze all the rigid grief of the actress. He had come to this apartment in order to solve her suicide.

**Murder.** Tallis stood behind the door of the lounge, shielded from the sunlight on the balcony, and considered the white cube of the room. At intervals Karen Novotny moved across it, carrying out a sequence of apparently random acts. Already she was confusing the perspectives of the room, transforming it into a dislocated clock. She noticed Tallis behind the door and walked towards him. Tallis waited for her to leave. Her figure interrupted the junction between the walls in the corner on his right. After a few seconds her presence became an unbearable intrusion into the time geometry of the room.

**Epiphany of this death.** Undisturbed, the walls of the apartment contained the serene face of the film star, the assuaged time of the dunes.

**Departure.** When Coma called at the apartment Tallis rose from his chair by Karen Novotny's body. 'Are you ready?' she asked. Tallis began to lower the blinds over the windows. 'I'll close these – no one may come here for a year.' Coma paced around the lounge. 'I saw the helicopter this morning – it didn't land.' Tallis disconnected the telephone behind the white leather desk. 'Perhaps Dr Nathan has given up.' Coma sat down beside Karen Novotny's body. She glanced at Tallis, who pointed to the corner. 'She was standing in the angle between the walls.'

*The Robing of the Bride.*
The title of one of Max Ernst's most mysterious paintings. An unseen woman is being prepared by two attendants for her marriage, and is dressed in an immense gown of red plumage that transforms her into a beautiful and threatening bird. Behind her, as if in a mirror, is a fossilized version of herself, fashioned from archaic red coral. All my respect and admiration of women is prompted by this painting, which I last saw at Peggy Guggenheim's museum in Venice, stared at by bored students. Leaving them, I strayed into a private corridor of the palazzo, and a maid emerging through a door with a vacuum cleaner gave me a glimpse into a bedroom overlooking the Grand Canal. Sitting rather sadly on the bed was Miss Guggenheim herself, sometime Alice at the surrealist tea-party, a former wife of Max Ernst, and by then an old woman. As she stared at the window I half-expected to see the bird costume on the floor beside her. She was certainly entitled to wear it.

*The 'Soft' Death of Marilyn Monroe.*
Marilyn Monroe's death was another psychic cataclysm. Here was the first and greatest of the new-style film goddesses, whose images, unlike those of their predecessors, were fashioned from something close to the truth, not from utter fiction. We know everything about Marilyn's sleazy past – the modest background, the foster homes and mother with mental problems, the long struggle as a starlet on the fringes of prostitution, then spectacular success as the world embraced her flawed charm, loved by sporting idols, intellectuals and, to cap it all, the US

61

President. But she killed herself, slamming the door in the world's face. Here Tallis, trying to make sense of her tragic death, has recast her disordered mind in the simplest terms possible, those of geometry: the shapes and volumes of the apartment house, the beach, the planetarium.

*Suite Mentale.*

The paintings of mental patients, like those of the surrealists, show remarkable insights into our notions of conventional reality, a largely artificial construct which serves the limited ambitions of our central nervous systems. Huge arrays of dampers suppress those perceptions that confuse or unsettle the central nervous system, and if these are bypassed, most dramatically by LSD, startling revelations soon begin to occur. In Springfield Mental Hospital near London a few years ago, while visiting a psychiatrist friend, I watched an elderly woman patient helping the orderly to serve the afternoon tea. As the thirty or so cups were set out on a large polished table she began to stare at the bobbing liquid, then stepped forward and carefully inverted the brimming cup in her hand. The hot liquid dripped everywhere in a terrible mess, and the orderly screamed: 'Doreen, why did you do that?', to which Doreen matter-of-factly replied: 'Jesus told me to.' She was right, though I like to think that what really impelled her was a sense of the intolerable contrast between the infinitely plastic liquid in her hand and the infinitely hard geometry of the table, followed by the revelation that she could resolve these opposites in a very simple and original way. She attributed the insight to divine intervention, but the order in fact came from some footloose conceptual area of her brain briefly waking from its heavy sleep of largactil.

Some of these transformational grammars I have tried to decode in the present book. Do the deaths of Kennedy and Marilyn Monroe, the space programme and the Vietnam war, the Reagan presidency make more sense seen in different terms? Perhaps. In 'You: Coma: Marilyn Monroe' the characters behave as if they were pieces of geometry interlocking in a series of mysterious equations.

*Impressions of Africa.*

Raymond Roussel (1877–1933), author of *Impressions of Africa* and *Locus Solus*, travelled with a coffin in which he would lie for a short time each day, preparing himself for death. Graveyards and cemeteries have the same calming effect, the more ornate the better. A visit to Père Lachaise in Paris adds a year to one's life, and the pyramids in Egypt stare down time itself. It would be intriguing to construct a mausoleum that was an exact replica, in the most funereal stone, of one's own home, even including the interior furniture (reminiscent of Magritte's strange stone paintings, with their stone men and women, stone trees and stone birds). One could weekend in this alternate home, and probably soon find oneself stepping out of time.

On the mortuary island of San Michele, in the Venice lagoon, a gloomy and threatening place that inspired Arnold Bocklin's 'Island of the Dead', one comes across an extraordinary parade of ultra-modern bungalows among the graves and tombs, with white walls and wrought iron grilles, like demonstration models of a Spanish-style nightclub waiting shipment to the Costa del Sol. These are family mausoleums, and it's touching to see the coffins sitting together in the breakfast rooms.

CHAPTER FIVE

## NOTES TOWARDS A MENTAL BREAKDOWN

**The Impact Zone.**  The tragic failure of these isolation tests, reluctantly devised by Trabert before his resignation, were to have bizarre consequences upon the future of the Institute and the already uneasy relationships between the members of the research staff. Catherine Austin stood in the doorway of Trabert's office, watching the reflection of the television screen flicker across the slides of exposed spinal levels. The magnified images of the newsreels from Cape Kennedy dappled the enamel walls and ceiling, transforming the darkened room into a huge cubicular screen. She stared at the transcriptions clipped to the memo board on Trabert's desk, listening to the barely audible murmur of the soundtrack. The announcer's voice became a commentary on the elusive sexuality of this strange man, on the false deaths of the three astronauts in the Apollo capsule, and on the eroded landscapes which the volunteers in the isolation tests had described so poignantly in their last transmissions.

**The Polite Wassermann.** Margaret Trabert lay on the blood-shot candlewick of the bedspread, unsure whether to dress now that Trabert had taken the torn flying jacket from his wardrobe. All day he had been listening to the news bulletins on the pirate stations, his eyes hidden behind the dark glasses as if deliberately concealing himself from the white walls of the apartment and its unsettled dimensions. He stood by the window with his back to her, playing with the photographs of the isolation volunteers. He looked down at her naked body, with its unique geometry of touch and feeling, as exposed now as the faces of the test subjects, codes of insoluble nightmares. The sense of her body's failure, like the incinerated musculatures of the three astronauts whose after-deaths were now being transmitted from Cape Kennedy, had dominated their last week together. He pointed to the pallid face of a young man whose photograph he had pinned above the bed like the icon of some algebraic magus. 'Kline, Coma, Xero – there was a fourth pilot on board the capsule. You've caught him in your womb.'

**The University of Death.** These erotic films, over which presided the mutilated figure of Ralph Nader, were screened above Dr Nathan's head as he moved along the lines of crashed cars. Illuminated by the arc-lights, the rushes of the test collisions defined the sexual ambiguities of the abandoned motorcade.

**Indicators of Sexual Arousal.** During the interval when the reels changed, Dr Nathan noticed that Trabert was peering at the photographs pinned to the windshields of the crashed cars. From the balcony of his empty office Catherine Austin watched him with barely focused eyes. Her leg stance, significant indicator of sexual arousal, confirmed all Dr Nathan had anticipated of Trabert's involvement with the events of Dealey Plaza. Behind him there was a shout from the camera crew. An enormous photograph of Jacqueline Kennedy had appeared in the empty rectangle of the screen. A bearded young man with an advanced neuro-muscular tremor in his lower legs stood in the brilliant pearl light, his laminated suit bathed in the magnified image of Mrs Kennedy's mouth. As he walked towards Trabert across the broken bodies of the plastic dummies, the screen jerked into a nexus of impacting cars, a soundless concertina of speed and violence.

**The Transition Area.** As Trabert prepared for his departure, the elements of apocalyptic landscapes waited on the horizons of his mind, helicopters burning among broken gantries. With deliberate caution, he waited in the empty apartment near the airport overpass, disengaging himself from the images of his wife, Catherine Austin and the patients at the Institute. Wearing his old flying jacket, he listened to the unending commentaries from Cape Kennedy – already he realized that the transmissions were coming from sources other than the television and radio stations. The deaths of the three astronauts in the Apollo capsule were a failure of the code that contained the operating formulae for their passage through consciousness. Many factors confirmed this faulty union of time and space – the dislocated perspectives of the apartment, his isolation from his own and his wife's body (he moved restlessly from one room to the next, as if unable to contain the volumes of his limbs and thorax), the serial deaths of Ralph Nader on the advertisement billboards that lined the airport approaches. Later, when he saw the young man in the laminated suit watching him from the abandoned amusement park, Trabert knew that the time had come for his rescue attempt: the resurrection of the dead spacemen.

**Algebra of the Sky.** At dawn Trabert found himself driving along an entry highway into the deserted city: terrain of shacks and filling stations, overhead wires like some forgotten algebra of the sky. When the helicopters appeared he left the car and set off on foot. Sirens wailing, white-doored squad cars screamed past him, neuronic icons on the spinal highway. Fifty yards ahead, the young man in the astronaut's suit plodded along the asphalt verge. Pursued by helicopters and strange police, they took refuge in an empty stadium. Sitting in the deserted stand, Trabert watched the young man pace at random around the pitch, replicating some meaningless labyrinth as if trying to focus his own identity. Outside Kline walked in the sculpture garden of the air terminal. His aloof, cerebral face warned Trabert that his rendezvous with Coma and Xero would soon take place.

**A Watching Trinity.** Personae of the unconscious: Xero: Run hot with a million programmes, this terrifying figure seemed to Trabert like a vast neural switchboard. During their time together, as he sat in the rear seat of the white Pontiac, he was never to see Xero's face, but fragments of his amplified voice reverberated among the deserted stands of the stadium, echoing through the departure bays of the air terminal.

Coma: This beautiful but mute young woman, madonna of the time-ways, surveyed Trabert with maternal eyes.

Kline: 'Why must we await, and fear, a disaster in space in order to understand our own time? – Matta.'

**The Karen Novotny Experience.** As she powdered herself after her bath, Karen Novotny watched Trabert kneeling on the floor of the lounge, surrounded by the litter of photographs like an eccentric Zen cameraman. Since their meeting at the emergency conference on Space Medicine he had done nothing but shuffle the photographs of wrecked capsules and automobiles, searching for one face among the mutilated victims. Almost without thinking she had picked him up in the basement cinema after the secret Apollo film, attracted by his exhausted eyes and the torn flying jacket with its Vietnam flashes. Was he a doctor, or a patient? Neither category seemed valid, nor for that matter mutually exclusive. Their period in the apartment together had been one of almost narcotic domesticity. In the planes of her body, in the contours of her breasts and thighs, he seemed to mimetize all his dreams and obsessions.

**Pentax Zoom.** In these equations, the gestures and postures of the young woman, Trabert explored the faulty dimensions of the space capsule, the lost geometry and volumetric time of the dead astronauts.

(1) Lateral section through the left axillary fossa of Karen Novotny, the elbow raised in a gesture of pique: the transliterated pudenda of Ralph Nader.

(2) A series of paintings of imaginary sexual organs. As he walked around the exhibition, conscious of Karen's hand gripping his wrist, Trabert searched for some valid point of junction. These obscene images, the headless creatures of nightmare, grimaced at him like the exposed corpses in the Apollo capsule, the victims of a thousand auto-crashes.

(3) 'The Stolen Mirror' (Max Ernst). In the eroded causeways and porous rock towers of this spinal landscape Trabert saw the blistered epithelium of the astronauts, the time-invaded skin of Karen Novotny.

**A Cosmogonic Venus.** Dr Nathan followed the young man in the laminated suit across the forecourt of the deserted air terminal. The metalled light shivered across the white steps like the defective image in a huge kinetic artifact. Unhurried, Dr Nathan stopped by the sculpture fountain to light a cigarette. He had been following the young man all morning, intrigued by the dialogue of motion and perspective played out in complete silence against the background of the air terminal. The young man looked back at Dr Nathan, as if waiting for him. A half-formed smile crossed his bruised mouth, revealing the scars of an automobile accident barely hidden by the pale beard. Dr Nathan gazed round at the forecourt. Someone had drained the ornamental pool. Like an immense uterus, its neck pointing towards the departure bays, it lay drying in the sunlight. The young man climbed the rim and walked down the sloping bowl to the centre. Dr Nathan laughed briefly into his gold-tipped cigarette. 'What a woman!' Perhaps Trabert would become her lover, tend her as she gave birth to the sky?

**The Abandoned Motorcade.** Walking through the deserted streets with Kline and Coma, Trabert found the motorcade abandoned in the sunlight. They moved along the rows of smashed cars, seating themselves at random beside the mannequins. Images of the Zapruder film hung on the fractured windshields, fusing with his dreams of Oswald and Nader. Somewhere the moving figure of a young man formed a plane of intersection. Later, by the drained swimming pool, he played with the life-sized plaster replicas of his wife and Karen Novotny. All week, to please Coma, he had studied the Zapruder frames, imitating the hairstyle of the President's widow. As the helicopter flew overhead its down-draught whirled at the matted wigs, driving into a cloud the photographs of

Marina Oswald, Madame Chiang and Mrs Kennedy which Trabert had laid out like a hand of patience on the floor of the pool.

**Operating Formulae.** Gesturing Catherine Austin into the chair beside his desk, Dr Nathan studied the elegant and mysterious advertisements which had appeared that afternoon in the copies of *Vogue* and *Paris-Match*. In sequence they advertised: (1) The left orbit and zygomatic arch of Marina Oswald. (2) The angle between two walls. (3) A 'neural interval' – a balcony unit on the twenty-seventh floor of the Hilton Hotel, London. (4) A pause in an unreported conversation outside an exhibition of photographs of automobile accidents. (5) The time, 11:47 a.m., June 23rd, 1975. (6) A gesture – a supine forearm extended across a candlewick bedspread. (7) A moment of recognition – a young woman's buccal pout and dilated eyes.

**'What exactly is he trying to sell?'** Ignoring Catherine Austin, Dr Nathan walked over to the photographs of the isolation volunteers on the enamel wall beside the window. The question revealed either astonishing ignorance or a complicity in that conspiracy of the unconscious he had only now begun to unravel. He turned to face the young woman, irritated as always by her strong, quizzical gaze, an overlay of her own potent sexuality. '*You*, Dr Austin. These advertisements constitute an explicit portrait of yourself, a contour map of your own body, an obscene newsreel of yourself during intercourse.' He rapped the magazines with his gold cigarette case. 'These images are fragments in a terminal moraine left behind by your passage through consciousness.'

**'Planes Intersect.'** Dr Nathan pointed to the photograph of a young man with a pale beard, the cast in his left eye displacing one side of his face. 'Planes intersect: on one level, the tragedies of Cape Kennedy and Vietnam serialized on billboards, random deaths mimetized in the experimental auto-disasters of Nader and his co-workers. Their precise role in the unconscious merits closer scrutiny, by the way; they may in fact play very different parts from the ones we assign them. On another level, the immediate personal environment, the volumes of space enclosed by your opposed hands, the geometry of your postures, the time-values contained in this office, the angles between these walls. On a third level, the inner world of the psyche. Where these planes intersect, images are born, some kind of valid reality begins to assert itself.'

**The Soft Quasars.**

Pre-uterine Claims – Kline.

'Young virgin auto-sodomized by her own chastity' – Coma.

Time-zones: Ralph Nader, Claude Eatherly, Abraham Zapruder.

**The Departure Platform.** Closer to this presiding trinity, Trabert waited among the departure bays in the deserted terminal. From the observation deck above the drained sculpture fountain, Coma watched him with her rune-filled eyes. Her broad cheekbones, reminiscent now of the President's widow, seemed to contain an immense glacial silence. On the roof terrace, Kline walked among the mannequins. The plaster models of Marina Oswald, Ralph Nader and the young man in the laminated suit stood by the railing. Xero, meanwhile, moved with galvanic energy across the runways, assembling an immense motorcade of wrecked cars. Behind the advance car, the Presidential limousine waited in the sunlight. The silence before a million auto deaths hung in the morning air.

**A Mere Modulus.** As Margaret Trabert hesitated among the passengers in the crowded departure building, Dr Nathan stepped behind her. His small face was dwarfed by the vast mural of a satellite capsule still drying on the wall above the escalators, the artist's trestles like a huge gantry that would carry the entire building into orbit. 'Mrs Trabert – don't you understand? This young woman with him is a mere modulus. His real target is yourself.' Irritated as always by Nathan, she brushed past the police detective who tried to block her way and ran into the forecourt. Among the thousands of cars in the parking lot she could see the white Pontiac. All week the young woman in the white car had been following her husband like some animal in rut.

**The Target Vehicle.** Dr Nathan pointed through the windshield with his cigarette. Two hundred yards ahead Margaret Trabert's car had turned out of a motel driveway. It set off along the deserted street, a white integer beneath the unravelling ciphers of the overhead wires. 'This motorcade,' Dr Nathan explained, 'we may interpret as a huge environmental tableau, a mobile psycho-drama which recapitulates the Apollo disaster in terms of both Dealey Plaza and the experimental car crashes examined so obsessively by Nader. In some way, presumably by a cathartic collision, Trabert will try to reintegrate space and so liberate the three men in the capsule. For him they still wait there on their contour couches.' As Catherine Austin touched his elbow he realized that he had lost sight of the white car.

**The Command Module.** Watched by Kline and Coma, Trabert moved behind the steering wheel of the open limousine. Behind the empty jump seats the plastic mannequins of the President and his wife sat in the rear of the car. As the motorcade moved off, Trabert peered through the frosted windshield. An immense target disc had been painted at the conjunction of the runways. From the departure area a white car turned on to the next runway and accelerated on a collision course towards the motorcade.

**Zapruder Frame 235.** Trabert waited until the audience had left the basement cinema. Holding in his hand the commercial replica of agent Greer's driving licence he had bought in the arcade near the overpass, he walked towards the young man sitting in the back row. Already his identity had begun to fade, the choreography of his hands tracing a last cipher across the blunted air.

**Epiphany of these Deaths.** The bodies of his wife and Karen Novotny lay on the floor of the empty swimming pool. In the carport Coma and Kline had taken their seats in the white Pontiac. Trabert watched them prepare to leave. At the last moment Coma seemed to hesitate, her broad mouth showing the scars on her lower lip. When they had gone, the helicopters rose from their waiting grounds along the highway. Trabert looked up as the sky was filled with these insane machines. Yet in the contours of his wife's thighs, in the dune-filled eyes of Karen

Novotny, he saw the assuaged time of the astronauts, the serene face of the President's widow.

**The Serial Angels.** Undisturbed now, the vaporizing figures of the dead astronauts diffused across the launching grounds, recreated in the leg stances of a hundred starlets, in a thousand bent auto fenders, in the million instalment deaths of the serial magazines.

*The Impact Zone.*
Little information has been released about the psychological effects of space travel, both on the astronauts and the public at large. Over the years NASA spokesmen have even denied that the astronauts dream at all during their space flights. But it is clear from the subsequently troubled careers of many of the astronauts (Armstrong, probably the only man for whom the 20th century will be remembered 50,000 years from now, refuses to discuss the moon-landing) that they suffered severe psychological damage. What did they dream about, how were their imaginations affected, their emotions and need for privacy, their perception of time and death? The Space Age lasted barely fifteen years, from Gagarin's first flight in 1961 to the first Apollo splashdown not shown live on TV in 1975, a consequence of the public's loss of interest – the brute-force ballistic technology is basically 19th century, as people realize, while advanced late-20th-century technologies are invisible and electronic-computers, microwave data links, faxes and VDUs are the stuff of which our dreams are made. Perhaps space travel is forever doomed because it inevitably recapitulates primitive stages in the growth of our nervous systems, before the development of our sense of balance and upright posture – a forced return to infantile dependency. Only intelligent machines may one day grasp the joys of space travel, seeing the motion sculpture of the space flights as immense geometric symphonies.

*The Transition Area.*
Here I see the disaster on the launch-pad at Cape Kennedy in terms of the most common dislocation of time and space the rest of us ever know – the car crash, and in particular the most extreme auto-disaster of our age, the motorcade assassination of JFK.

*Algebra of the Sky.*
'Neuronic icons on the spinal highway.' Here, as throughout *The Atrocity Exhibition*, the nervous systems of the characters have been externalized, as part of the reversal of the interior and exterior worlds. Highways, office blocks,faces and street signs are perceived as if they were elements in a malfunctioning central nervous system.

*A Watching Trinity.*
The Chilean painter, Roberto Matta, one of the last of the surrealists, asked this as yet unanswerable question. All disasters – earthquakes, plane or car crashes – seem to reveal for a brief moment the secret formulae of the world around us, but a disaster in space rewrites the rules of the continuum itself.

*Pentax Zoom.*
The flattening effect of the zoom lens reduces everything to a two-dimensional world, eliminating the sense of time. Years ago, while on holiday in Greece, I would borrow my son's telescope and gaze at the town across the Bay of Argos. People were clearly visible, but none of them seemed to move, although the resort was in fact a hive of holiday-makers and busy traffic.

*Operating Formulae.*
At the time of writing I was publishing my series of paid advertisements in *Ambit* and other magazines (see *Re/Search #8/9*, pages 148–52). One of these, 'The Angle Between Two Walls', actually appeared as the second of the series, a still from Steve Dwoskin's film *Alone*, about

a woman masturbating. Sadly, I ran out of cash, and my half-serious application to the Arts Council for a grant (I asked for funds to pay for ads in *Time* and the American *Vogue*) was turned down. I can't remember the significance of 11:47 a.m. on a June day in 1975, then some eight years ahead. As it happens I was probably reading the *International Herald-Trib* on a Spanish beach and wondering how to escape from England altogether.

*The Soft Quasars.*
'Young virgin auto-sodomised by her own chastity.' One of Dali's most original paintings. The notion of an attractive woman being ravished by her own beauty is familiar to us all, but here Dali convinces us purely in terms of the body's geometry.

## CHAPTER SIX

# THE GREAT AMERICAN NUDE

**The Skin Area.** Each morning, during this last phase of Talbert's work at the Institute, Catherine Austin was conscious of the increasing dissociation of the events around her. As she entered the projection theatre the noise of the soundtrack reverberated across the sculpture garden, a melancholy tocsin modulated by Talbert's less and less coherent commentary. In the darkness she could see the group of paretic patients sitting between their nurses in the front row. All week they had watched the montaged sequences of commercial pornographic films, listening without response to Talbert's analysis of each posture and junction. Catherine Austin stared at the giant frames. Fossilized into the screen, the terraced images of breast and buttock had ceased to carry any meaning. His face and suit dappled by the projector, Talbert leaned against the screen, as if bored by his own exposition. Every evening he examined the barely legible questionnaires, apparently searching for a pointer to his own behaviour, the key to a new sexuality. As the lights came on she buttoned her white coat, suddenly conscious of her body.

**The New Eros.** From the window of his office, Dr Nathan watched Talbert standing on the roof of the multi-storey car park. The deserted deck was a favourite perch. The inclined floors seemed a model of Talbert's oblique

79

personality, forever meeting the events of time and space at an invisible angle. Aware of Catherine Austin fidgeting beside him, Dr Nathan lit a gold-tipped cigarette. A young woman in a white tennis dress was walking towards the sculpture garden. Talbert's eyes followed her like a voyeur's. Already he had built up a substantial collection of erotica. What new junction would he find in the sex act?

**A Diagram of Bones.** Talbert stopped at the entrance to the sculpture garden. Programmes in hand, the students wandered among the exhibits, staring at the truncated segments of coloured plastic tubing, the geometry of a Disney. From the smiling young woman at the open-air desk he accepted a programme. On its cover was printed a fragment of a half-familiar face, an enlarged detail of the left orbit of a film actress. Here and there on the lawn the students were fitting together the frames. Where would the pubis lie? The young woman in the white dress walked among the fractured profiles of Mia Farrow and Elizabeth Taylor.

**The See-Through Brain.** Throwing away her programme, Karen Novotny hurried towards the entrance of the car park. The white American car had followed her around the perimeter of the sculpture garden, always fifty yards behind. She turned on to the ramp leading to the first floor. As the car stopped at the pay kiosk she recognized the man behind the wheel. All week this hunched figure with his high forehead and insane sunglasses had been photographing her with his cine camera. To her annoyance he had even inserted zooms from the film in his little festival of dirty movies – no doubt his psychotic patients had ejaculated into their strait-jackets. When she reached the roof the white car cruised towards her. Out of breath, she leaned against the parapet. Talbert gazed at her with an almost benign curiosity, his eyes exploring the templates of her face. One arm hung over the driving door, as if about to touch her thighs. He was holding her discarded programme. He raised the fragment against her left breast, matching the diameters of cleavage and nipple.

**Profane Marriage.** As they left the projection theatre a dark-bearded young man stood by a truck outside. He was supervising the unloading of a large tableau sculpture, a Segal showing a man and woman during intercourse in a bath. Karen seized his arm. 'Talbert – they're you and I . . .' Irritated by yet another of the research student's ominous pranks, Talbert walked over to Koester. His eyes were like those of a nervous priest about to officiate at a profane marriage.

**A History of Nothing.** Narrative elements: a week of hunting the overpasses, the exploration of countless apartments. With stove and sleeping-bag, they camped like explorers on the sitting-room floors. 'They're exhibits, Karen – *this* conception will be immaculate.' Later they raced around the city, examining a dozen architectures. Talbert pushed her against walls and parapets, draped her along balustrades. In the rear seat the textbooks of erotica formed an encyclopedia of postures – blueprints for her own imminent marriage with a seventh-floor balcony unit of the Hilton Hotel.

 Amatory elements: nil. The act of love became a vector in an applied geometry. She could barely touch his shoulders without galvanizing him into a spasm of activity. Some scanning device in his brain had lost a bolt. Later, in the dashboard locker she found a set of maps of the Pripet Marshes, a contour photogram of an armpit, and a hundred publicity stills of the screen actress.

**Landscapes of the Dream.** Various landscapes preoccupied Talbert during this period: (1) The melancholy back of the Yangtse, a boom of sunken freighters off the Shanghai Bund. As a child he rowed out to the rusting ships, waded through saloons awash with water. Through the portholes, a regatta of corpses sailed past Woosung Pier. (2) The contours of his mother's body, landscape of so many psychic capitulations. (3) His son's face at the moment of birth, its phantom-like profile older than Pharaoh. (4) The death-rictus of a young woman. (5) The breasts of the screen actress. In these landscapes lay a key.

**Baby Dolls.** Catherine Austin stared at the objects on Talbert's desk. These flaccid globes, like the obscene sculptures of Bellmer, reminded her of elements of her own body transformed into a series of imaginary sexual organs. She touched the pallid neoprene, marking the vents and folds with a broken nail. In some weird way they would coalesce, giving birth to deformed sections of her lips and armpit, the junction of thigh and perineum.

**A Nervous Bride.** At the gates of the film studio Dr Nathan handed his pass to the guard. 'Stage H,' he said to Koester. 'Apparently it was rented by someone at the Institute three months ago. At a nominal charge, fortunately – most of the studio is disused now.' Koester parked the car outside the empty production offices. They walked through into the stage. An enormous geometric construction filled the hangar-like building, a maze of white plastic convolutions. Two painters were spraying pink lacquer over the bulbous curves. 'What is this?' Koester asked with irritation. 'A model of $\sqrt{-1}$?' Dr Nathan hummed to himself. 'Almost,' he replied coolly. 'In fact, you're looking at a famous face and body, an extension of Miss Taylor into a private dimension. The most tender act of love will take place in this bridal suite, the celebration of a unique nuptial occasion. And why not? Duchamp's nude shivered her way downstairs, far more desirable to us than the Rokeby Venus, and for good reason.'

**Auto-Zoomar.** Talbert knelt in the *a tergo* posture, his palms touching the wing-like shoulder blades of the young woman. A conceptual flight. At ten-second intervals the Polaroid projected a photograph on to the screen beside the bed. He watched the auto-zoom close in on the union of their thighs and hips. Details of the face and body of the film actress appeared on the screen, mimetized elements of the planetarium they had visited that morning. Soon the parallax would close, establishing the equivalent geometry of the sexual act with the junctions of this wall and ceiling.

**'Not in the Literal Sense.'** Conscious of Catherine Austin's nervous hips as she stood beside him, Dr Nathan studied the photograph of the young woman. 'Karen Novotny,' he read off the caption. 'Dr Austin, may I assure you that the prognosis is hardly favourable for Miss Novotny. As far as Talbert is concerned the young woman is a mere modulus in his union with the film actress.' With kindly eyes he looked up at Catherine Austin. 'Surely it's self-evident – Talbert's intention is to have intercourse with Miss Taylor, though needless to say not in the literal sense of that term.'

**Action Sequence.** Hiding among the traffic in the near-side lane, Koester followed the white Pontiac along the highway. When they turned into the studio entrance he left his car among the pines and climbed through the perimeter fence. In the shooting stage Talbert was staring through a series of colour transparencies. Karen Novotny waited passively beside him, her hands held like limp birds. As they grappled he could feel the exploding muscu-lature of Talbert's shoulders. A flurry of heavy blows beat him to the floor. Vomiting through his bloodied lips, he saw Talbert run after the young woman as she darted towards the car.

**The Sex Kit.** 'In a sense,' Dr Nathan explained to Koester, 'one may regard this as a kit, which Talbert has devised, entitled "Karen Novotny" – it might even be feasible to market it commercially. It contains the following items: (1) Pad of pubic hair, (2) a latex face mask, (3) six detach-able mouths, (4) a set of smiles, (5) a pair of breasts, left nipple marked by a small ulcer, (6) a set of non-chafe orifices, (7) photo cut-outs of a number of narrative situ-ations – the girl doing this and that, (8) a list of dialogue samples, of inane chatter, (9) a set of noise levels, (10) descriptive techniques for a variety of sex acts, (11) a torn anal detrusor muscle, (12) a glossary of idioms and catch phrases, (13) an analysis of odour traces (from various vents), mostly purines, etc., (14) a chart of body tempera-tures (axillary, buccal, rectal), (15) slides of vaginal

84

smears, chiefly Ortho-Gynol jelly, (16) a set of blood pressures, systolic 120, diastolic 70 rising to 200/150 at onset of orgasm . . .' Deferring to Koester, Dr Nathan put down the typescript. 'There are one or two other bits and pieces, but together the inventory is an adequate picture of a woman, who could easily be reconstituted from it. In fact, such a list may well be more stimulating than the real thing. Now that sex is becoming more and more a conceptual act, an intellectualization divorced from affect and physiology alike, one has to bear in mind the positive merits of the sexual perversions. Talbert's library of cheap photo-pornography is in fact a vital literature, a kindling of the few taste buds left in the jaded palates of our so-called sexuality.'

**A Helicopter Flight.** As they sped along the highway the young woman flinched against the door pillar, eyes fixed on the huge trucks swaying beside them. Talbert put his arm around her, pulling her on to his shoulder. He steered the heavy car with one hand, swinging it off the motorway towards the airfield. 'Relax, Karen.' In a mimicry of Dr Nathan's voice, he added, 'You're a mere modulus, my dear.' He looked down at the translucent skin over the anterior triangle of her neck, barely hiding its scenarios of nerve and blood-vessel. Marker lines sped past them, dividing and turning. The helicopter waited below the ruined control tower. He pulled her from the car, then buttoned his flying jacket around her shoulders.

**The Primary Act.** As they entered the cinema, Dr Nathan confided to Captain Webster, 'Talbert has accepted in absolute terms the logic of the sexual union. For him all junctions, whether of our own soft biologies or the hard geometries of these walls and ceilings, are equivalent to one another. What Talbert is searching for is the primary act of intercourse, the first apposition of the dimensions of time and space. In the multiplied body of the film actress – one of the few valid landscapes of our age – he finds what seems to be a neutral ground. For the most part the phenomenology of the world is a nightmarish excrescence. Our bodies, for example, are for him monstrous extensions of puffy tissue he can barely tolerate. The inventory of the young woman is in reality a death kit.' Webster watched the images of the young woman on the screen, sections of her body intercut with pieces of modern architecture. All these buildings. What did Talbert want to do – sodomize the Festival Hall?

**Pressure Points.** Koester ran towards the road as the helicopter roared overhead, its fans churning up a storm of pine needles and cigarette cartons. He shouted at Catherine Austin, who was squatting on the nylon blanket, steering her body stocking around her waist. Two hundred yards beyond the pines was the perimeter fence. She followed Koester along the verge, the pressure of his hands and loins still marking her body. These zones formed an inventory as sterile as the items in Talbert's kit. With a smile she watched Koester trip clumsily over a discarded tyre. This unattractive and obsessed young man – why had she made love to him? Perhaps, like Koester, she was merely a vector in Talbert's dreams.

**Central Casting.** Dr Nathan edged unsteadily along the catwalk, waiting until Webster had reached the next section. He looked down at the huge geometric structure that occupied the central lot of the studio, now serving as the labyrinth in an elegant film version of *The Minotaur*. In a sequel to *Faustus* and *The Shrew*, the film actress and her husband would play Ariadne and Theseus. In a remarkable way the structure resembled her body, an exact formalization of each curve and cleavage. Indeed, the technicians had already christened it 'Elizabeth'. He steadied himself on the wooden rail as the helicopter appeared above the pines and sped towards them. So the Daedalus in this neural drama had at last arrived.

**An Unpleasant Orifice.** Shielding his eyes, Webster pushed through the camera crew. He stared up at the young woman standing on the roof of the maze, helplessly trying to hide her naked body behind her slim hands. Eyeing her pleasantly, Webster debated whether to climb on to the structure, but the chances of breaking a leg and falling into some unpleasant orifice seemed too great. He stood back as a bearded young man with a tight mouth and eyes ran forwards. Meanwhile Talbert strolled in the centre of the maze, oblivious of the crowd below, calmly waiting to see if the young woman could break the code of this immense body. All too clearly there had been a serious piece of miscasting.

**'Alternate' Death.** The helicopter was burning briskly. As the fuel tank exploded, Dr Nathan stumbled across the cables. The aircraft had fallen on to the edge of the maze, crushing one of the cameras. A cascade of foam poured over the heads of the retreating technicians, boiling on the hot concrete around the helicopter. The body of the young woman lay beside the controls like a figure in a tableau sculpture, the foam forming a white fleece around her naked shoulders.

**Geometry of Guilt.** Later, when the studio was deserted, Dr Nathan saw Talbert standing on the roof of the maze, surveying the contours of the sloping basin below. His dark-skinned face resembled that of a pensive architect. Once again Karen Novotny had died, Talbert's fears and obsessions mimetized in her alternate death. Dr Nathan decided not to speak to him. His own identity would seem little more than a summary of postures, the geometry of an accusation.

**Exposed Placenta.** The following week, when Dr Nathan returned, Talbert had not moved. He sat on the edge of the water-filled basin, staring into the lucid depths of that exposed placenta. His emaciated figure was by now little more than a collection of tatters. After watching him for half an hour Dr Nathan walked back to his car.

*The Great American Nude.*
'The Great American Nude' is the running title of a series of paintings by the Pop artist Tom Wesselman, which rework the iconic possibilities of the commercial nude. As with much of Pop art, the bland surface defuses the subject, making an unsettling comment on our notions of fame and celebrity.

*A Diagram of Bones.*
All over the world major museums have bowed to the influence of Disney and become theme parks in their own right. The past, whether Renaissance Italy or ancient Egypt, is reassimilated and homogenized into its most digestible form. Desperate for the new, but disappointed with anything but the familiar, we recolonize past and future. The same trend can be seen in personal relationships, in the way people are expected to package themselves, their emotions and sexuality in attractive and instantly appealing forms.

*Profane Marriage.*

An imaginary Segal, as far as I know. His plaster figures scarcely lend themselves to sexual activity, perhaps because they have effectively died under the ash of their future Pompeii.

*Landscapes of the Dream.*

The many lists in *The Atrocity Exhibition* were in effect free-association tests. What I find surprising after so many years is how they anticipate the future themes of my fiction. Item 1 shows my wartime experiences in Shanghai surfacing briefly, before disappearing again for nearly two decades. Heaven alone knows what will surface in the future.

*Baby Dolls.*

Hans Bellmer's work is now totally out of fashion, hovering as it does on the edge of child pornography. Yet it's difficult to imagine any paedophile being excited by his strange dolls and dainty, Alice-like little girls with their reversed orifices and paradoxical anatomy. But his vision is far too close for comfort to the truth.

*'Not in the Literal Sense.'*

'Needless to say . . .' Certainly needless by this stage, if the reader has been giving even a tenth of his attention to the text. Dr Nathan represents the safe and sane voice of the sciences. His commentaries are accurate, and he knows what is going on. On the other hand, reason rationalizes reality for him, as it does for the rest of us, in the Freudian sense of providing a more palatable or convenient explanation, and there are so many subjects today about which we should not be reasonable.

*The Sex Kit.*

Sex, which many enthusiasts in the 1960s thought they had invented, then seemed to be the new frontier, though AIDS has recently cooled our ardour. Even so, the mass media publicly offer a range of options which previously have been available only in private. Thanks to press, film and television, sex has become a communal and public activity for the first time since the Edens of a more primitive age. In a sense we now all take part in sex whether we want to or not. Many people, like the characters in *The Atrocity Exhibition*, use sex as a calculated means of exploring uncertainties in their make-up, exploiting the imaginative possibilities that sex provides. Any sex act can become a nerve-wracking psycho-drama in which one is recruited into someone else's company of players. Dimestore de Sades stalk the bedrooms of suburbia, re-enacting the traumas of weaning and potty training. The test of a language is how well it can be translated into other tongues, and sex is the most negotiable language of all.

*Central Casting.*
Elizabeth Taylor and Richard Burton had appeared in stage versions of *Faustus* and *The Taming of the Shrew*, typecasting for both, especially Burton, who had the look in his last years of a man who had made the devil's bargain and knew he had lost — but drunk or sober, he was always interesting and sympathetic.

*'Alternate' Death.*
'Alternate Deaths' occur again and again in *The Atrocity Exhibition*. By these I mean the re-enactment of various tragedies staged by Traven and his many selves. They take place partly in his own mind and partly in the external world, and represent his attempt to make sense of these unhappy events and attribute to them a moral dimension and even, perhaps, a measure of hope. In Traven's mind Kennedy and Monroe have 'died', but not yet been laid to rest.

## CHAPTER SEVEN

## THE SUMMER CANNIBALS

**Locus Solus.** Through the dust-covered windscreen she watched him walk along the beach. Despite the heat he had been wandering about by himself for half an hour, as if following an invisible contour inside his head. After their long drive he had stopped on this isthmus of clinker only a few hundred yards from their apartment. She closed the novel lying on her knees, took out her compact and examined the small ulcer on her lower lip. Exhausted by the sun, the resort was almost deserted – beaches of white pumice, a few bars, apartment blocks in ice-cream colours. She looked up at the shutters, thinking of the sun-blackened bodies sprawled together in the darkness, as inert as the joints of meat on supermarket counters. She closed the compact. At last he was walking back to the car, an odd-shaped stone in one hand. A fine ash like milled bone covered his suit. She placed her arm on the window-sill. Before she could move the hot cellulose stung her skin.

**The Yes or No of the Borderzone.** Between the aluminium grilles of the balcony he could see the banks of the drained river half a mile away, piers of collapsing sand like the ruined columns of an ornamental canal. He turned his head on the pillow, following the white flex of a power cable as it angled its way around the bedroom door. A manoeuvre of remarkable chasteness. He listened to the water jet against the frosted panes of the shower stall. As the door opened the blurred profile of her body took on a sudden liquid focus, moving across the bedroom like a pink meniscus. She took a cigarette from his packet, then flashed the lighter in her preoccupied eyes. Head in a towel, she lay on the bedspread, smoking the wet cigarette.

**B-Movie.** He sat at the glass-topped table beside the news stand, watching the young woman pick through the copies of *Oggi* and *Paris-Match*. Her face, with its unintelligent eyes and pearl lips whispering like a child's, was reflected in the stereotypes of a dozen magazine covers. He finished his drink and followed her through the arcade, curious to see her reaction. In the deserted open-air cinema she unlatched the door of the pay kiosk and locked it behind herself with a rusty key. Why on earth had he followed her? Suddenly bored by the young woman, he climbed the concrete aisle and walked among the empty seats, staring at the curved screen. She turned the pages of her magazine, watching him over her shoulder.

**Love among the Mannequins.** Unable to move, he lay on his back, feeling the sharp corner of the novel cut into his ribs. Her hand rested across his chest, nails holding the hair between his nipples like a lover's scalp brought back for him as a trophy. He looked at her body. Humped against his right shoulder, her breasts formed a pair of deformed globes like the elements of a Bellmer sculpture. Perhaps an obscene version of her body would form a more significant geometry, an anatomy of triggers? In his eye, without thinking, he married her right knee and left breast, ankle and perineum, armpit and buttock.

Carefully, to avoid waking her, he eased his arm from beneath her head. Through the apartment window the opalescent screen of the open-air cinema rose above the rooftops. Immense fragments of Bardot's magnified body illuminated the night air.

**A Confusion of Mathematical Models.** Holding her cheap Nikon, he led the young woman down the bank. In the sunlight the drained river stretched below them, a broken chequerboard floor. At its mouth a delta of shingle formed an ocean bar, pools of warm water filled with sea urchins. Beyond the silver span of the motor bridge lay basins of cracked mud the size of ballrooms – models of a state of mind, a curvilinear labyrinth. Handing her the camera, he began to explore the hollows around them. Images of Bardot's body seemed to lie in these indentations, deformed elements of thigh and thorax, obscene sexual wounds. Fingering the shaving scar on his jaw, he watched the young woman waiting with her back to him. Already, without touching her, he knew intimately the repertory of her body, its anthology of junctions. His eyes turned to the multi-storey car park beside the apartment blocks above the beach. Its inclined floors contained an operating formula for their passage through consciousness.

**Soft Geometry.** The audience's laughter drummed against the walls of the cubicle behind the pay kiosk, dislodging a carton of automat tickets from the shelf above his head. He pushed it back with one hand, finding with the other a small mole on her left shoulder blade like a minuscule nipple. Strangely surprised by even this blemish on her otherwise under-pigmented skin, he bent down and touched it with his lips. She watched him with a tired smile, the same rictus that had fixed itself on her mouth during their afternoon in the dusty heat trap below the bank. Was he playing an elaborate game with her, using their acts of intercourse for some perverse pleasure of his own? In many ways her body retraced the contours they had explored together. Above the window of the cubicle fluttered the reverse image of the cinema screen, Bardot's translucent face twisted into a bizarre pout.

**Non-Communicating Dialogue.** As he entered the apartment she was sitting on the balcony, painting her nails. Drying in the sunlight beside her was the novel he had thrown into the bidet, its pages flowering into an elegant ruff. She looked up from her nail file. 'Did you enjoy the film?' He walked into the bathroom, wincing at himself in the mirror, that always more tired older brother. The half-hearted inflection of irony in her voice no longer irritated him. An enormous neutral ground now divided them, across which their emotions signalled like meaningless semaphores. If anything, her voice formed a module with the perspectives of wall and ceiling as abstract as the design on a detergent pack. She sat down beside him on the bed, splaying her wet nails in a gesture of intimacy. He stared at the transverse scar above her navel. What act between them would provide a point of junction?

**A Krafft-Ebing of Geometry and Posture.** He remembered these pleasures: the conjunction of her exposed pubis with the polished contours of the bidet; the white cube of the bathroom quantifying her left breast as she bent over the handbasin; the mysterious eroticism of the multi-storey car park, a Krafft-Ebing of geometry and posture; her flattened thighs on the tiles of the swimming pool below; her right hand touching the finger-smeared panel of the elevator control. Looking at her from the bed, he re-created these situations, conceptualizations of exquisite games.

**The Solarium.** Beyond the café tables the beach was deserted, the white pumice fossilizing the heat and sunlight. He played with the beer mat, shaping the cigarette ash on the tables into a series of small pyramids. She waited behind her magazine, now and then flicking at the fly in her citrus juice. He pulled at the damp crotch of his trousers. On an impulse, as they lay in the small room near the car park, he had dressed and taken her down to the café, fed up with her chronic cystitis and sore urethra. For hours his hands had searched her passive flesh, hunting for some concealed key to their sexuality. He traced the contours of breast and pelvis inside the yellow linen dress, then looked round as a young man walked towards them through the empty tables.

**Imaginary Perversions.** He tipped the warm swill from his glass on to the ash-stained sand. '. . . it's an interesting question – in *what* way is intercourse per vagina more stimulating than with this ashtray, say, or with the angle between two walls? Sex is now a conceptual act, it's probably only in terms of the perversions that we can make contact with each other at all. Sexual perversions are morally neutral, cut off from any suggestion of psycho-pathology – in fact, most of the ones I've tried are out of date. We need to invent a series of imaginary sexual perversions just to keep our feelings alive . . .' The girl's attention strayed to her magazine and then to the young

95

man's sunburned wrist. The handsome loop of his gold bracelet swung above her knee. As he listened, the young man's uncritical eyes were sharpened by moments of humour and curiosity. An hour later, when she had left him, he saw them talking together by the kiosk of the open-air cinema.

**An Erotic Game.** 'Have we stopped?' Waving at the dust that filled the cabin, she waited patiently as he worked away at the steering wheel. The road had come to a dead end among the ashy dunes. On the rear window ledge the novel had opened and begun to curl again in the heat like a Japanese flower. Around them lay portions of the drained river, hollows filled with pebbles and garbage, the remains of steel scaffolding. Yet their position in relation to the river was uncertain. All afternoon they had been following this absurd sexual whim of his, plunging in and out of basins of dust, tracking across beds of mud like nightmare chessboards. Overhead was the concrete span of the motor bridge, its arch as ambiguously placed as a rainbow's. She looked up wearily from her compact as he spoke. 'You drive.'

**Elements of an Orgasm.** (1) Her ungainly transit across the passenger seat through the nearside door; (2) the conjunction of aluminized gutter trim with the volumes of her thighs; (3) the crushing of her left breast by the door pillar, its self-extension as she swung her legs on to the sandy floor; (4) the overlay of her knees and the metal door flank; (5) the ellipsoid erasure of dust as her hip brushed the nearside fender; (6) the hard transept of the door mechanism within the absolute erosion of the landscape; (7) her movements distorted in the projecting carapace of the radiator assembly; (8) the conjunction of her thighs with the arch of the motor bridge, the contrast of smooth epithelium and corrugated concrete; (9) her weak ankles in the soft ash; (10) the pressure of her right hand on the chromium trim of the inboard head-lamp; (11) the sweat forming a damp canopy in the cleavage of her blouse – the entire landscape expired within this irrigated trench; (12) the jut and rake of her pubis as she moved into the driving seat; (13) the junction of her thighs and the steering assembly; (14) the movements of her fingers across the chromium-tipped instrument heads.

**Post-coitum Triste.** He sat in the darkened bedroom, listening to her cleaning the shower stall. 'Do you want a drink? We could go down to the beach.' He ignored her voice, with its unconvinced attempt at intimacy. Her movements formed a sound body like a nervous bird's. Through the window he could see the screen of the open-air cinema, and beyond it the canted decks of the multi-storey car park.

**Foreplay.** Above the pay kiosk the sections of shoulder and abdomen shifted across the screen, illuminating the late afternoon sky. He waited in the arcade behind a wall of wicker baskets. As they left the cubicle beside the kiosk he followed them towards the car park. The angular floors rose through the fading light, the concrete flanks lit by the neon signs of the bars across the street. As they drove from the town the first billboard appeared – Cinemascope of breast and thigh, deceit and need terraced in the contours of the landscape. In the distance was the silver span of the motor bridge. The lunar basin of the river lay below.

**Contours of Desire.** In the dusk light he studied the contours of the embankment. The concrete caissons sank through the discoloured sand, forming lines of intersection whose focus was the young woman stepping from the parked car. Headlamps sped towards him. Without thinking, he drove across the road into the oncoming lane. The perspectives of the landscape shifted with the changing camber.

**Some Bloody Accident.** She stared at the blood on her legs. The heavy liquid pulled at her skirt. She stepped over the shirtless body lying across a car seat and vomited on to the oily sand. She wiped the phlegm from her knees. The bruise under her left breast reached behind her sternum, seizing like a hand at her heart. Her bag lay beside an overturned car. At the second attempt she picked it up, and climbed with it on to the road. In the fading light the silver girders of the motor bridge led towards the beach and a line of billboards. She ran clumsily along the road, eyes fixed on the illuminated screen of the open-air cinema, while the huge shapes disgorged themselves across the rooftops.

**Love Scene.** Steering with one hand, he followed the running figure along the bridge. In the darkness he could see her broad hips lit by the glare of the headlamps. Once she looked back at him, then ran on when he stopped fifty yards from her and reversed the car. He switched off the headlamps and moved forward, steering from side to side as he varied her position against the roadside hoardings, against the screen of the open-air cinema and the inclined floor of the multi-storey car park.

**Zone of Nothing.** She took off her Polaroid glasses. In the sunlight the oil spattered across the windscreen formed greasy rainbows. As she waited for him to return from the beach she wiped her wrists with a cologne pad from the suitcase in the rear seat. What was he doing? After his little affairs he seemed to enter a strange zone. A young man in red trunks came up the track, arching his toes in the hot sand. Deliberately he leaned against the car as he walked by, staring at her and almost touching her elbow. She ignored him without embarrassment. When he had gone she looked down at the imprints of his feet in the white pumice. The fine sand poured into the hollows, a transfer of geometry as delicate as a series of whispers. Unsettled, she put away her novel and took the newspaper from the dashboard locker. She studied the photographs of an automobile accident – overturned cars, bodies on ambulance trolleys, a bedraggled girl. Five minutes later he climbed into the car. Thinking of the photographs, she put her hand on his lap, watching the last of the footprints vanish in the sand.

*Locus Solus.*
Named after another work by Raymond Roussel, the locus solus might be Miami Beach, but in fact is a generalized vision of San Juan, near Alicante in Spain, where I once pushed my tank-like Armstrong-Siddeley to 100 mph on the beach road, and where my wife died in 1964. The curious atmosphere of the Mediterranean beach resorts still awaits its chronicler. One could regard them collectively as a linear city, some 3000 miles long, from Gibraltar to Glyfada beach north of Athens, and 300 yards deep. For three summer months the largest city in the world, population at least 50 million, or perhaps twice that. The usual hierarchies and conventions are absent; in many ways it couldn't be less

European, but it works. It has a unique ambience – nothing, in my brief experience, like Venice, California, or Malibu. At present it is Europe's Florida, an endless parade of hotels, marinas and apartment houses, haunted by criminals running hash from North Africa, stealing antiquities or on the lam from Scotland Yard.

Could it ever become Europe's California? Perhaps, but the peculiar geometry of those identical apartment houses seems to defuse the millenarian spirit. Living there, one is aware of the exact volumes of these generally white apartments and hotel rooms. After the more sombre light of northern Europe, they seem to focus an intense self-consciousness on the occupants. Sex becomes stylized, relationships more oblique. The office workers and secretaries all behave like petty criminals vaguely on the run, so many topless Janet Leighs who have decided *not* to take that shower and can't remember where they left their lives. The growing numbers of full-time residents seem almost decorticated. My dream is to move there permanently. But perhaps I already have.

During beach holidays I devour foreign-language news magazines, though I can't speak a word of French, Italian or Spanish, and always rent a TV set. In England I watch most TV with the sound turned down, but in France or Spain I boost the volume, particularly of news bulletins. A study of hijackers revealed that they are generally poor linguists (and often suffer from vestibular disturbances of the inner ear, the balancing organ – perhaps the hijack is in part an unconscious attempt to cure the defect). They prefer not to understand what is going on around them, so they can impose their own subjective image upon the external world – a trait common to all psychotics.

*Soft Geometry.*
The white light has bleached out the identities of the characters, even deleting their names (reminding me a little of Miami Beach, where no one seemed to know who they were, realizing that it no longer mat-tered). This is Traven again, or a saner version of himself, veering

between his wife and the young woman who works at the open-air movie theatre, but a Traven devoid of those larger concerns that preoccupy him elsewhere in the book.

### A Krafft-Ebing of Geometry and Posture.
These mental Polaroids form a large part of our library of affections. Carried around in our heads, they touch our memories like albums of family photographs. Turning their pages, we see what seems to be a ghostly and alternative version of our own past, filled with shadowy figures as formalized as Egyptian tomb-reliefs.

### Imaginary Perversions.
Traven has a point, and the process may receive an unhappy impetus from AIDS. It's hard to visualize, but the day may come when genital sex is a seriously life-threatening health hazard (not for the first time, when one thinks of 19th-century syphilis – the Goncourt brothers' journal resembles the last years of the Warhol diaries). At that point the imagination may claim the sexual impulse as its own, an inheritance wholly free of any biological entail. As always with such inheritances, there will be any number of new friends eager to help in its spending.

### Elements of an Orgasm.
The sex act is emotionally the richest and the most imaginatively charged event in our lives, comparable only to the embrace of our children as a source of affection and mystery. But no kinaesthetic language has yet been devised to describe it in detail, and without one we are in the position of an unqualified observer viewing an operation for brain surgery. Ballet, gymnastics, American football and judo are furnished with elaborate kinaesthetic languages, but it's still easier to describe the tango or the cockpit take-off procedures for a 747 than to recount in detail an act of love.

101

## CHAPTER EIGHT

# TOLERANCES OF THE HUMAN FACE

**Five Minutes 3 Seconds.** Later, Travers remembered the camera crew which had visited the Institute, and the unusual documentary they had filmed among the cypress-screened lawns. He had first noticed the unit as he loaded his suitcases into the car on the afternoon he resigned. Avoiding Catherine Austin's embarrassed attempt to embrace him, he stepped on to the lawn below the drive. The patients sat like mannequins on the worn grass, while the film crew moved between them, guiding the camera about like a myopic robot. 'Why did Nathan invite them here? For a so-called documentary on dementia praecox it's going to be surprisingly elegant and perverse.' Catherine Austin strode towards the unit, remonstrating with the director as he pointed a woman patient towards the camera. She took the girl's loose hands. The director stared at her in a bored way, deliberately exposing the chewing gum between his lips. His eyes turned to inspect Travers. With an odd gesture of the wrist, he beckoned the camera unit forward.

**Hidden Faces.** Travers vaulted over the concrete balustrade and pushed through the swing doors of the lecture theatre. Behind him the film crew were manhandling their camera trolley across the gravel. Hands on the hips of his white safari suit the director watched Travers with his

103

unpleasant eyes. His aggressive stare had surprised Travers – seeing himself confused with the psychotic patients was too sharp a commentary on his own role at the Institute, a reminder of his long and wearisome dispute with Nathan. In more than one sense he had already left the Institute; the presence of his colleagues, their smallest gestures, formed an anthology of irritations. Only the patients left him at ease. He crossed the empty seats below the screen. *Each afternoon in the deserted cinema Travers was increasingly distressed by the images of colliding motor cars. Celebrations of his wife's death, the slow-motion newsreels recapitulated all his memories of childhood, the realization of dreams which even during the safe immobility of sleep would develop into nightmares of anxiety.* He made his way through the exit into the car park. His secretary's car waited by the freight elevator. He touched the dented fender, feeling the reversed contours, the ambiguous junction of rust and enamel, geometry of aggression and desire.

**Fake Newsreels.**  Catherine Austin unlocked the door and followed Travers into the deserted laboratory. 'Nathan did warn me not to . . .' Ignoring her, Travers walked towards the display screens. Disconnected headphones hung inside the cubicles, once occupied by the volunteer panels of students and housewives. Fingers fretting at the key in her pocket, she watched Travers search through the montage photographs which the volunteers had assembled during anaesthesia. Disquieting diorama of pain and mutilation: strange sexual wounds, imaginary Vietnam atrocities, the deformed mouth of Jacqueline Kennedy. Until Nathan ordered the experiment to end it had become a daily nightmare for her, a sick game which the volunteers had increasingly enjoyed. Why was Travers obsessed by these images? Their own sexual relationship was marked by an almost seraphic tenderness, transits of touch and feeling as serene as the movements of a dune.

**From the Casualty Ward.** Nostalgia of departure. Through the windshield Travers glanced for the last time at the window of his office. The glass curtain-walling formed an element in a vertical sky, a mirror of this deteriorating landscape. As he released the handbrake a young man in a shabby flying jacket strode towards the car from the freight elevator. He fumbled at the door, concentrating on the latch mechanism like a psychotic patient struggling with a spoon. He sat down heavily beside Travers, beckoning at the steering wheel with a gesture of sudden authority. Travers stared at the flame-like scars on his knuckles, residues of an appalling act of violence. This former day-patient, Vaughan, he had often seen in the back row of his classes, or moving through the other students in the library forecourt at some private diagonal. His committal to the Institute, an elaborate manoeuvre by Nathan, had been a first warning. Should he help Vaughan to escape? The dented plates of his forehead and the sallow jaw were features as anonymous as any police suspect's. The musculature of his mouth was clamped together in a rictus of aggression, as if he were about to commit a crude and unsavoury crime. Before Travers could speak, Vaughan brushed his arm aside and switched on the ignition.

**Hard Edge.** Dr Nathan gestured to the young woman to unbutton her coat. With a murmur of surprise he stared at the bruises on her hips and buttocks. 'Travers . . . ?' He turned to Catherine Austin, standing primly by the window. Nodding to himself, he searched the broken

105

blood-vessels in the young woman's skin. She showed no hostility to Travers, at first sight an indication of the sexual nature of these wounds. Yet something about the precise cross-hatching suggested that their true role lay elsewhere. He waited by the window as the young woman dressed. 'What these girls carry about under their smiles – you saw her little art gallery?' Catherine Austin snapped shut the roller blind. 'They're hardly in Travers's style. Do you believe her?' Dr Nathan gestured irritably. 'Of course. That's the whole point. He was trying to make contact with her, but in a new way.' A car moved down the drive. He handed the girl a jar of ointment, happy to be present at a vernissage no larger than the skin area of a typist.

**Veteran of the Private Evacuations.** Ahead, stalled traffic blocked three lanes. Oxyacetylene flared over the roofs of the police cars and ambulances in a corral at the mouth of the underpass. Travers rested his head against the mud-caked quarter-window. He had spent the past days in a nexus of endless highways, a terrain of billboards, car marts and undisclosed destinations. Deliberately he had allowed Vaughan to take command, curious to see where they would go, what junction points they would cross on the spinal causeways. Together they set off on a grotesque itinerary: a radio-observatory, stock car races, war graves, multi-storey car parks. Two teenage girls whom they picked up Vaughan had almost raped, grappling with them in a series of stylized holds. During this exercise in the back seat his morose eyes had stared at Travers through the driving mirror with a deliberate irony imitated from the newsreels of Oswald and Sirhan. Once, as they walked along the half-built embankment of a new motorway, Travers had turned to find Vaughan watching

106

him with an expression of almost insane lucidity. His presence sounded a tocsin of danger and violence. Soon after, Travers became bored with the experiment. At the next filling station, while Vaughan was in the urinal, he drove off alone.

**Actual Size.** A helicopter clattered overhead, a cameraman crouched in the bubble cockpit. It circled the overturned truck, then pulled away and hovered above the three wrecked cars on the verge. Zooms for some new Jacopetti, the elegant declensions of serialized violence. Travers started the engine and turned across the central reservation. As he drove off he heard the helicopter climb away from the accident site. It soared over the motorway, the shadows of its blades scrambling across the concrete like the legs of an ungainly insect. Travers swerved into the nearside lane. Three hundred yards ahead he plunged down the incline of a slip road. As the helicopter circled and dived again he recognized the white-suited man crouched between the pilot and the camera operator.

**Tolerances of the Human Face in Crash Impacts.** Travers took the glass of whisky from Karen Novotny. 'Who is Koester? – the crash on the motorway was a decoy. Half the time we're moving about in other people's games.' He followed her on to the balcony. The evening traffic turned along the outer circle of the park. The past few days had formed a pleasant no-man's land, a dead zone on the clock. As she took his arm in a domestic gesture he looked at her for the first time in half an hour. This strange young woman, moving in a complex of undefined roles, the gun moll of intellectual hoodlums with her art critical jargon and bizarre magazine subscriptions. He had met her in the demonstration cinema during the interval, immediately aware that she would form the perfect subject for the re-enactment he had conceived. What were she and her fey crowd doing at a conference on facial surgery? No doubt the lectures were listed in the diary pages of *Vogue*, with the professors of tropical diseases as popular with their claques as fashionable hairdressers. 'What about you, Karen? – wouldn't you like to be in the movies?' With a stiff forefinger she explored the knuckle of his wrist. 'We're all in the movies.'

**The Death of Affect.** He parked the car among the over-luminous pines. They stepped out and walked through the ferns to the embankment. The motorway moved down a cut, spanned by a concrete bridge, then divided through the trees. Travers helped her on to the asphalt verge. As she watched, face hidden behind the white fur collar, he began to pace out the trajectories. Five minutes later he beckoned her forward. 'The impact point was here – roll-over followed by head-on collision.' He stared at the surface of the concrete. After four years the oil stains had vanished. These infrequent visits, dictated by what-ever private logic, now seemed to provide nothing. An immense internal silence presided over this area of cement and pines, a terminal moraine of the emotions that held its debris of memory and regret, like the rubbish in the pockets of a dead schoolboy he had examined. He felt Karen touch his arm. She was staring at the culvert between bridge and motorway, an elegant conjunction of rain-washed concrete forming a huge motion sculpture. Without thinking, she asked, 'Where did the car go?' He led her across the asphalt, watching as she re-created the accident in terms of its alternate parameters. How would she have preferred it: in terms of the Baltimore-Washington Parkway, the '50s school of highway engineering or, most soigné of all, the Embarcadero Freeway?

**The Six-Second Epic.** Travers waited on the mezzanine terrace for the audience to leave the gallery floor. The Jacopetti retrospective had been a success. As the crowd cleared, he recognized the organizer, a now-familiar figure in his shabby flying jacket, standing by a display of Biafran atrocity photographs. Since his reappearance two weeks earlier Vaughan had taken part in a string of modish activities: police brawls, a festival of masochistic films, an obscene play consisting of a nine-year-old girl in a Marie Antoinette dress watching a couple in intercourse. His involvement in these lugubrious pastimes seemed an elaborate gesture, part of some desperate irony. His hostility to Karen Novotny, registered within a few seconds of their first meeting, reflected this same abstraction of emotion and intent. Even now, as he waved to Karen and Travers, his eyes were set in a canny appraisal of her hoped-for wound areas. More and more Travers found himself exposing Karen to him whenever possible.

**A New Algebra.** 'Travers asked you to collect these for him?' Dr Nathan looked down at the photostats which Catherine Austin had placed on his desk: (1) Front elevation of multi-storey car park; (2) mean intra-patellar distances (estimated during funeral services) of Coretta King and Ethel M. Kennedy; (3) close-up of the perineum of a six-year-old girl; (4) voice-print (terminal transmission) of Col. Komarov on the record jacket of a commercial 45; (5) the text of 'Tolerances of the Human Face in Crash Impacts'. Dr Nathan pushed away the tray, shaking his head. '"Fusing Devices" –? God only knows what violence Vaughan is planning – it looks as if Koester's film may have a surprise ending.'

**Madonna of the Multi-Storey Car Park.** She lay on her side, waiting as his hands explored the musculature of her pelvis and abdomen. From the TV set came a newsreel of a tank crushing a bamboo hut, for some reason an effort of immense labour. American combat engineers were staring like intelligent tourists at an earth bunker. For days the whole world had been in slow motion. Travers had become more and more withdrawn, driving her along the motorway to pointless destinations, setting up private experiments whose purpose was totally abstract: making love to soundless images of war newsreels, swerving at speed through multi-storey car parks (their canted floors appeared to be a model of her own anatomy), leading on the mysterious film crew who followed them everywhere. (What lay behind the antagonism between Travers and the unpleasant young director – some sort of homo-erotic jealousy, or another game?) She remembered the wearying hours outside the art school, as he waited in the car, offering money to any student who would come back to the apartment and watch them in intercourse. Travers had embarked on the invention of imaginary psychopathologies, using her body and reflexes as a module for a series of unsavoury routines, as if hoping in this way to recapitulate his wife's death. With a grimace she thought of Vaughan, for ever waiting for them at unexpected junctions. In his face the diagram of bones formed a geometry of murder.

**Internal Emigré.** All afternoon they had driven along the highway. Moving steadily through the traffic, Travers followed the white car with the fractured windshield. Now and then he would see Vaughan's angular forehead, with its depressed temples, as the young man looked back over his shoulder. They left the city and entered a landscape of pines and small lakes. Vaughan stopped among the trees in a side road. Striding swiftly in his tennis shoes, he set off across the soft floor of pine needles. Travers drew up beside his car. Strange graffiti marked the dust on its trunk and door panels. He followed Vaughan around the shore of an enclosed lake. Over the densely packed trees lay a calm and unvarying light. A large exhibition hall appeared above the forest, part of a complex of buildings on the edge of a university campus. Vaughan crossed the lawn towards the glass door. As Travers left the shelter of the trees he heard the roar of a helicopter's engine. It soared overhead, the down-draught from its blades whipping his tie across his eyes. Driven back, he traced his steps through the pines. For the next hour he waited by the lake shore.

**Cinecity.** In the evening air Travers passed unnoticed through the crowd on the terrace. The helicopter rested on the lawn, its blades drooping over the damp grass. Through the glass doors Travers could see into the festival arena, where a circle of cine screens carried their films above the heads of the audience. Travers walked around the rear gangway, now and then joining in the applause, interested to watch these students and middle-aged cinephiles. Endlessly, the films unwound: images of neuro-surgery and organ transplants, autism and senile dementia, auto-disasters and plane crashes. Above all, the montage landscapes of war and death: newsreels from the Congo and Vietnam, execution squad instruction films, a

111

documentary on the operation of a lethal chamber. *Sequence in slow motion: a landscape of highways and embankments, evening light on fading concrete, intercut with images of a young woman's body. She lay on her back, her wounded face stressed like fractured ice. With almost dream-like calm, the camera explored her bruised mouth, the thighs dressed in a dark lace-work of blood. The quickening geometry of her body, its terraces of pain and sexuality, became a source of intense excitement. Watching from the embankment, Travers found himself thinking of the eager deaths of his childhood.*

**Too Bad.** Of this early period of his life, Travers wrote: 'Two weeks after the end of World War II my parents and I left Lunghua internment camp and returned to our house in Shanghai, which had been occupied by the Japanese gendarmerie. The four servants and ourselves were still without any food. Soon after, the house opposite was taken over by two senior American officers, who gave us canned food and medicines. I struck up a friendship with their driver, Corporal Tulloch, who often took me around with him. In October the two colonels flew to Chungking. Tulloch asked me if I would like to go to Japan with him. He had been offered a round trip to Osaka by a quartermaster-sergeant at the Park Hotel occupation head-quarters. My father was away on business, my mother too ill to give any thought to the question. The skies were full of American aircraft flying to and from Japan. We left the next afternoon, but instead of going to the Nantao airfield we set off for Hongkew riverfront. Tulloch told me we would go by L.C.T. Japan was 500 miles away, the journey would take only a few days. The wharves were crammed with American landing craft and supply vessels as we drove through Hongkew. On the mudflats at

Yangtzepoo were the huge stockades where the Americans held the last of the Japanese troops being repatriated. As we arrived four L.C.T.s were beached on the bank. A line of Japanese soldiers in ragged uniforms moved along a bamboo pier to the loading ramp. Our own L.C.T. was already loaded. With a group of American servicemen we climbed the stern gangway and went to the forward rail above the cargo well. Below, crammed shoulder-to-shoulder, were some four hundred Japanese, squatting on the deck and looking up at us. The smell was intense. We went to the stern, where Tulloch and the others played cards and I read through old copies of *Life* magazine. After two hours, when the L.C.T.s next to us had set off down-river, an argument broke out between the officers in charge of our ship and the military personnel guarding the Japanese. For some reason we would have to leave the next morning. Packing up, we went by truck back to Shanghai. The next day I waited for Tulloch outside the Park Hotel. Finally he came out and told me that there had been a delay. He sent me off home and said he would collect me the following morning. We finally set off again in the early afternoon. To my relief, the L.C.T. was still berthed on the mudflat. The stockades were empty. Two navy tenders were tied up at the stern of the L.C.T. The deck was crowded with passengers already aboard, who shouted at us as we climbed the gangway. Finally Tulloch and I found a place below the bridge rail. The Japanese soldiers in the cargo well were in bad condition. Many were lying down, unable to move. An hour later a landing craft came alongside. Tulloch told me that we were all to transfer to a supply ship leaving on the next tide. As we climbed down into the landing craft two Eurasian women and myself were turned away. Tulloch shouted at me to go back to the Park Hotel. At this point one of the soldiers guarding the Japanese called me back on board. He told me that they would be leaving shortly and that I could go with them. I sat at the stern, watching the landing craft cross the river. The Eurasian women walked back to the shore across the mudflats. At eight o'clock that night a fight broke out among the Americans. A Japanese sergeant was standing on the bridge deck, his face and chest covered with blood, while the Americans shouted and pushed at each other. Shortly after, three trucks drove up and a party of armed American military police came on board. When they saw me they told me to leave. I left the ship and walked back through the darkness to the empty stockades. The trucks were loaded with gasoline drums. A week later my father returned. He took me on the Mollar line ferry to the cotton mill he owned on the Pootung shore, two miles down-river from the Bund. As we passed Yangtzepoo the L.C.T. was still on the mudflat. The forward section of the ship had been set on fire. The sides were black, and heavy smoke still rose from the cargo well. Armed military police were standing on the mudflat.'

**'Homage to Abraham Zapruder.'** Each night, as Travers moved through the deserted auditorium, the films of simulated atrocities played above the rows of empty seats, images of napalm victims, crashing cars and motorcade attacks. Travers followed Vaughan from one projection theatre to the next, taking his seat a few rows behind him. When a party in evening dress came in Travers followed him on to the library floor. As Vaughan leafed through the magazines he listened to the flow of small talk, the suave ironies of Koester and his women. Koester had a face like a fake newsreel.

114

**Go, No-Go Detector.** These deaths preoccupied Travers. *Malcolm X:* the death of terminal fibrillation, as elegant as the trembling of hands in tabes dorsalis; *Jayne Mansfield:* the death of the erotic junction, the polite section of the lower mammary curvature by the glass guillotine of the windshield assembly; *Marilyn Monroe:* the death of her moist loins; the falling temperature of her rectum embodied in the white rectilinear walls of the twentieth-century apartment; *Jacqueline Kennedy:* the notional death, defined by the exquisite eroticism of her mouth and the logic of her leg stance; *Buddy Holly:* the capped teeth of the dead pop singer, like the melancholy dolmens of the Brittany coastline, were globes of milk, condensations of his sleeping mind.

**The Sex Deaths of Karen Novotny.** The projection theatre was silent as the last film began. Travers recognized the figures on the screen – Dr Nathan, Catherine Austin, himself. In sequence the rushes of the sex deaths of Karen Novotny passed before them. Travers stared at the young woman's face, excited by these images of her postures and musculature and the fantasies of violence he had seen in the imaginary newsreels.

**The Dream Scenario.** As Travers walked through the pines towards his car he recognized Karen Novotny sitting behind the wheel, fur collar buttoned round her chin. The white strap of her binocular case lay above the dashboard. The fresh scent of the pine needles irrigated his veins. He opened the door and took his seat in the passenger compartment. 'Where have you been?' Travers studied her body, the junction of her broad thighs with the vinyl seat cover, her nervous fingers moving across the chromium instrument heads.

**Conceptual Games.** Dr Nathan pondered the list on his desk-pad. (1) The catalogue of an exhibition of tropical diseases at the Wellcome Museum; (2) chemical and topographical analyses of a young woman's excrement; (3) diagrams of female orifices: buccal, orbital, anal, urethral, some showing wound areas; (4) the results of a questionnaire in which a volunteer panel of parents were asked to devise ways of killing their own children; (5) an item entitled 'self-disgust' – someone's morbid and hate-filled list of his faults. Dr Nathan inhaled carefully on his gold-tipped cigarette. Were these items in some conceptual game? To Catherine Austin, waiting as ever by the window, he said, 'Should we warn Miss Novotny?'

**Biomorphic Horror.** With an effort, Dr Nathan looked away from Catherine Austin as she picked at her finger quicks. Unsure whether she was listening to him, he continued: 'Travers's problem is how to come to terms with the violence that has pursued his life – not merely the violence of accident and bereavement, or the horrors of war, but the biomorphic horror of our own bodies. Travers has at last realized that the real significance of these acts of violence lies elsewhere, in what we might term "the death of affect". Consider our most real and tender pleasures – in the excitements of pain and mutilation; in sex as the perfect arena, like a culture-bed of sterile pus, for all the veronicas of our own perversions, in voyeurism and self-disgust, in our moral freedom to pursue our own psychopathologies as a game, and in our ever greater powers of abstraction. What our children have to fear are not the cars on the freeways of tomorrow, but our own pleasure in calculating the most elegant parameters of their deaths. The only way we can make contact with each other is in terms of conceptualiz-ations. Violence is the conceptualization of pain. By the same token psychopathology is the conceptual system of sex.'

**Sink Speeds.** During this period, after his return to Karen Novotny's apartment, Travers was busy with the following projects: a cogent defence of the documentary films of Jacopetti; a contribution to a magazine symposium on the optimum auto-disaster; the preparation, at a for-mer colleague's invitation, of the forensic notes to the catalogue of an exhibition of imaginary genital organs. Immersed in these topics, Travers moved from art gallery to conference hall. Beside him, Karen Novotny seemed more and more isolated by these excursions. Advertise-ments of the film of her death had appeared in the movie magazines and on the walls of the underground stations. 'Games, Karen,' Travers reassured her. 'Next they'll have you filmed masturbating by a cripple in a wheel chair.'

**Imaginary Diseases.** By contrast, for Catherine Austin these activities were evidence of an ever widening despair, a deliberate summoning of the random and grotesque. After their meeting at the exhibition Travers grasped her arm so tightly that his fingers bruised a nerve. To calm him, she read through the catalogue introduction: 'Bernouli's *Encyclopedia of Imaginary Diseases* was compiled during his period as a *privat-dozent* in Frankfurt. Beginning with the imaginary diseases of the larynx, he proceeded to a number of fictional malfunctions of the respiratory and cardiovascular systems. Within a few years, as he added the cerebro-spinal system to his encyclopedia, a substantial

117

invented pathology had been catalogued. Bernouli's monographs on imaginary defects of speech are a classic of their period, equalled only by his series of imaginary diseases of the bladder and anus. His greatest work without doubt is his exhaustive "imaginary diseases of the genitalia" – his concept of the imaginary venereal disease represents a tour de force of extraordinary persuasion. A curious aspect of Bernouli's work, and one that must not be overlooked, is the way in which the most bizarre of his imaginary diseases, those which stand at the summit of his art and imagination, in fact closely approximate to conditions of natural pathology . . .'

**Marriage of Freud and Euclid.** These embraces of Travers's were gestures of displaced affections, a deformed marriage of Freud and Euclid. Catherine Austin sat on the edge of the bed, waiting as his hands moved across her left armpit, exploring the parameters of a speculative geometry. In a film magazine on the floor were a series of photographs of a young woman's death postures, stills from Koester's unsavoury documentary. These peculiar geometric elements contained within them the possibilities of an ugly violence. Why had Travers invited her to this apartment above the zoo? The traces of a young woman's body clung to its furniture – the scent on the bedspread, the crushed contraceptive wallet in the desk drawer, the intimate algebra of pillow arrangements. He worked away endlessly on his obscene photographs: left breasts, the grimaces of filling station personnel, wound areas, catalogues of Japanese erotic films: 'targeting areas', as he described them. He seemed to turn everything into its inherent pornographic possibilities. She grimaced as he grasped her left nipple between thumb and forefinger;

an obscene manual hold, part of a new grammar of callousness and aggression. Koester's eyes had moved across her body in the same transits when she blundered into the film crew outside the multi-storey car park. Vaughan had stood on the parapet beside the crashed car, staring down at her with cold and stylized rapacity.

**Death Games (a) Conceptual.** Looking back at his wife's death, Travers now reconceived it as a series of conceptual games: (1) a stage show, entitled 'Crash'; (2) a volume curve in a new transfinite geometry; (3) an inflatable kapok sculpture two hundred yards long; (4) a slide show of rectal cancers; (5) six advertisements placed in *Vogue* and *Harper's Bazaar*; (6) a board game; (7) a child's paper-doll books, cut-out tabs mounted around the wound areas; (8) the notional 'pudenda' of Ralph Nader; (9) a set of noise levels; (10) a random collection of dialogue samples, preserved on videotape, from ambulance attendants and police engineers.

**Death Games (b) Vietnam.** Dr Nathan gestured at the war newsreels transmitted from the television set. Catherine Austin watched from the radiator panel, arms folded across her breasts. 'Any great human tragedy – Vietnam, let us say – can be considered experimentally as a larger model of a mental crisis mimetized in faulty stair angles or skin junctions, breakdowns in the perception of environment and consciousness. In terms of television and the news magazines the war in Vietnam has a latent significance very different from its manifest content. Far from repelling us, it *appeals* to us by virtue of its complex of polyperverse acts. We must bear in mind, however sadly, that psychopathology is no longer the exclusive preserve of the degenerate and perverse. The Congo, Vietnam, Biafra – these are games that anyone can play. Their violence, and all violence for that matter, reflects the neutral exploration of sensation that is taking place now, within sex as elsewhere, and the sense that the perversions are valuable precisely because they provide a readily accessible anthology of exploratory techniques. Where all this leads one can only speculate – why not, for example, use our own children for all kinds of obscene games? Given that we can only make contact with each other through the new alphabet of sensation and violence, the death of a child or, on a larger scale, the war in Vietnam, should be regarded as for the public good.' Dr Nathan stopped to light a cigarette. 'Sex, of course, remains our continuing preoccupation. As you and I know, the act of intercourse is now always a model for something else. What will follow is the psychopathology of sex, relationships so lunar and abstract that people will become mere extensions of the geometries of situations. This will allow the exploration, without any taint of guilt, of every aspect of sexual psychopathology. Travers, for example, has composed a series of new sexual deviations, of a wholly conceptual character, in an attempt to surmount this death of affect. In many ways he is the first of the new naives, a Douanier Rousseau of the sexual perversions. However consoling, it seems likely that our familiar perversions will soon come to an end, if only because their equivalents are too readily available in strange stair angles, in the mysterious eroticism of overpasses, in distortions of gesture and posture. At the logic of fashion, such once-popular perversions as paedophilia and sodomy will become derided clichés, as amusing as pottery ducks on suburban walls.'

**Chase Sequence.** As the helicopter roared over their heads again, Travers and Karen Novotny ran towards the shelter of the overpass. Karen stumbled over a wooden trestle, falling across the concrete. She held her bloodied left palm up to Travers, her face in a grimace of stupidity. Travers took her arm and pulled her on to the unset cement between the pillars of the overpass. The cleats of Vaughan's tennis shoes had left a line of imprints ahead of them, tracks which they were helplessly following. Vaughan was stalking them like the nemesis of some over-lit dream, always in front of them as they tried to escape from the motorway. Travers stopped and pushed Karen to the ground. The helicopter was coming after them below the deck of the overpass, blades almost touching the pillars, like an express train through a tunnel. Through the bubble canopy he could see Koester crouched between the pilot and cameraman.

**Che as Pre-Pubertal Figure.** *Travers stood awkwardly in front of the student volunteers. With an effort, he began: 'The imaginary sex-death of Che Guevara – very little is known about Guevara's sexual behaviour. Psychotic patients, and panels of housewives and filling station personnel were asked to construct six alternate sex-deaths. Each of these takes place within some kind of perversion – for example, bondage and concentration camp fantasies, auto-deaths, the obsessive geometry of walls and ceilings. Some suggestions have been made for considering Che as a pre-pubertal figure. Patients have been asked to consider the notional "child-rape" of Che Guevara . . .' Travers stopped, aware for the first time of the young man sitting in the back row. Soon he would have to break with Vaughan. In his dreams each night Karen Novotny would appear, showing her wounds to him.*

**'What are you thinking about?'** Travers walked along the embankment of the overpass. The concrete slope ran on into the afternoon haze. Karen Novotny followed a few steps behind him, absently picking at the spurs of grass in her skirt. 'An erotic film – of a special kind.' Somewhere in the margins of his mind a helicopter circled, vector in a scenario of violence and desire. He counted the materials of the landscape: the curvilinear perspectives of the concrete causeways, the symmetry of car fenders, the contours of Karen's thighs and pelvis, her uncertain smile. What new algebra would make sense of these elements? As the haze cleared he saw the profile of the multi-storey car park rising above them. A familiar figure in a shabby flying jacket watched from the roof. Travers let Karen walk past him. As she sauntered along the verge he became aware of a sudden erotic conjunction, the module formed by Vaughan, the inclined concrete decks and Karen's body. Above all, the multi-storey car park was a model for her rape.

**Treblinka.** Cement dust rose from the wheels of the approaching car. Travers held Karen's arm. He pointed to the ramp. 'Go up to the roof. I'll see you there later.' As she set off he ran into the road, signalling to the driver. Through the windshield he could see Catherine Austin's knuckles on the steering wheel, Dr Nathan cupping his ears for the sounds of the helicopter. As Catherine Austin reversed and drove the heavy sedan down the slip road Travers walked back to the car park. After a pause he strolled towards the stairway.

**The Film of Her Death.** Dr Nathan pushed back the metal door of the elevator head. Before stepping into the overheated sunlight on the roof he nursed the bruise on his left ankle. Vaughan had burst from the elevator doors like an ugly animal sprung from a trap. The noise of the helicopter's engine had faded fractionally. Shielding his head from the down-draught, he stepped on to the roof. The aircraft was rising vertically, its camera trained on the body of a young woman lying in the centre of the deck. The black bilateral parking lines formed a complex diagonal structure around her. Holding his throat with one hand, Dr Nathan stared at the body. He turned to look behind him. Travers was standing by the elevator head, gazing at the body on the white concrete slope, jetsam of this terminal beach. Nodding to Nathan, he walked to the elevator.

**Last Summer.** For Travers, these afternoons in the deserted cinema were periods of calm and rest, of a reappraisal of the events which had brought him to the multi-storey car park. Above all, these images from Koester's film reminded him of his affection for the young woman, discovered after so many disappointments within the darkness of this projection theatre. At the conclusion of the film he would go out into the crowded streets. The noisy traffic mediated an exquisite and undying eroticism.

*Tolerances of the Human Face.*
The resonant title of this chapter I owe entirely to my girlfriend Claire Churchill (who formed the subject of my first advertisement – see *Re/ Search #8/9*, page 148). Working at a London publisher's office in the late 1960s, she came across a scientific paper, 'Tolerances of the Human Face in Crash Impacts', and realized that here was a title waiting for its rendezvous with a Ballard fiction.

*Fake Newsreels.*

Bizarre experiments are now a commonplace of scientific research, moving ever closer to that junction where science and pornography will eventually meet and fuse. Conceivably, the day will come when science is itself the greatest producer of pornography. The weird perversions of human behaviour triggered by psychologists testing the effects of pain, isolation, anger, etc., will play the same role that the bare breasts of Polynesian islanders performed in 1940s wildlife documentary films.

*From the Casualty Ward.*

A first appearance of Vaughan, who was later to appear as the 'hoodlum scientist' in *Crash*.

*Actual Size.*

Jacopetti's *Mondo Cane* series of documentary films enjoyed a huge vogue in the 1960s. They cunningly mixed genuine film of atrocities, religious cults and 'Believe-it-or-not' examples of human oddity with carefully faked footage. The fake war newsreel (and most war newsreels are faked to some extent, usually filmed on manoeuvres) has always intrigued me – my version of *Platoon, Full Metal Jacket* or *All Quiet on the Western Front* would be a newsreel compilation so artfully faked as to convince the audience that it was real, while at the same time reminding them that it might be wholly contrived. The great Italian neo-realist, Roberto Rossellini, drew close to this in *Open City* and *Paisa*.

*Tolerances of the Human Face in Crash Impacts.*

In the 1890s the most fashionable surgeons in London did indeed have their claques of society ladies present in the operating theatre.

*The Six-Second Epic.*

In the early 1950s a part-time prostitute who occupied the room next to mine in a Notting Hill hotel would dress her little daughter in a Marie Antoinette costume, along with gilded hat and silk umbrella. She was always present when the clients climbed the high staircase, and I nearly alerted the police, assuming these gloomy, middle-aged men had sex with the child. But a woman neighbour assured me that all was well – during sex with the mother they were merely watched by the child. Before I could do anything they had moved. This was Christie-land.

*A New Algebra.*
The Russian astronaut Col. Komarov was the first man to die in space, though earlier fatalities had been rumoured. Komarov is reported to have panicked when his space-craft began to tumble uncontrollably, but the transcripts of his final transmissions have never been released. I'm sceptical of what may be NASA-inspired disinformation. The courage of professional flight-crews under extreme pressure is clearly shown in *The Black Box*, edited by Malcolm MacPherson, which contains cockpit voice-recorder transcripts in the last moments before airliner crashes. The supreme courage and stoicism shown by these men and women in the final seconds running up to their deaths, as they wrestle with the collapsing systems of their stricken aircraft, is a fine memorial to them, and a powerful argument for equal frankness in other areas.

*Cinecity.*
Our TV sets provided an endless background of frightening and challenging images – the Kennedy assassination, Vietnam, the Congo civil war, the space programme – each seeming to catalyse the others, and all raising huge questions which have never been answered. Together they paved the landscape of the present day, and provide the ambiguous materials of this book, in which I have tried to identify what I see as the hidden agendas. Also, clearly, my younger self was hoping to understand his wife's meaningless death. Nature's betrayal of this young woman seemed to be mimicked in the larger ambiguities to which the modern world was so eager to give birth, and its finish line was that death of affect, the lack of feeling, which seemed inseparable from the communications landscape.

*Too Bad.*
'The fateful question for the human species seems to me to be whether and to what extent their cultural development will succeed in mastering the disturbance of their communal life by the human instinct of aggression and self-destruction. It may be that in this respect precisely the present time deserves a special interest. Men have gained control over the forces of nature to such an extent that with their help they would have no difficulty in exterminating one another to the last man. They know this, and hence comes a large part of their current unease, their unhappiness and mood of anxiety. And now it is to be expected that the other of the two "Heavenly Powers", eternal Eros, will make an effort to assert himself in the struggle with his equally immortal adversary. But who can foresee with what success and with what result?' – Sigmund Freud, *Civilisation and Its Discontents*.


*'Homage to Abraham Zapruder.'*
The violent newsreel footage shown on TV in the 1960s has now been censored from our screens, though a certain sexual frankness struggles on. Housewives strip on Italian game shows, sections of French television seem to be permanently topless, while call-girls star in thirty-second amateur versions of *Blue Velvet* on New York's Channel 23. The last must be among the most reductive of all films, featuring a bed, a woman, and an incitement to lust, usually filmed in a weird and glaucous blue, an individual's entire reason for existence compressed into these desperate moments. By contrast the professionally produced ads for the large escort agencies are as inspiring as commercials for a new hotel chain. Needless to say, I believe there should be more sex and violence on TV, not less. Both are powerful catalysts for change, in areas where change is urgent and overdue.


*Conceptual Games.*
'After reading Edgar Allan Poe. Something the critics have not noticed: a new literary world pointing to the literature of the 20th century.

126

Scientific miracles, fables on the pattern A + B; a clear-sighted, sickly literature. No more poetry but analytic fantasy. Something mono-maniacal. Things playing a more important part than people; love giving way to deductions and other sources of ideas, style, subject and interest. The basis of the novel transferred from the heart to the head, from the passion to the idea, from the drama to the denouement.'

*The Goncourt Brothers' Journal*, July 16, 1856.

*Imaginary Diseases.*

'Bernouli's *Encyclopedia of Imaginary Diseases*.' My own invention, but some deranged pathologist might already have anticipated me. Physicians are capable of far more eccentricity than their patients realize, as Dr Benway, William Burroughs's brilliant creation, illustrates in *Naked Lunch*. Given their generally phlegmatic nature, this seems surprising. As a medical student dissecting cadavers, I remember thinking: 'These rather dull men and women will have reached the summit of their profession forty years from now, just when I start to need their help.' Presumably the unequalled richness of their source material propels their imagina-tions along unexpected paths. Doctors have remarkably high suicide rates, perhaps a consequence of long-term imposed depression and easy access to lethal drugs. Psychiatrists, unsurprisingly, show the highest rate, paediatricians and surgeons (the latter the most worldly and ambitious of all) the lowest. The bizarre *Bulletin of Suicidology* in an early 1970s issue analysed US physicians' favourite methods that year, from the most popular, lethal injection, to the rarest, two deaths by deliber-ately crashed light aircraft.

*Death Games (a) Conceptual.*

Nader again. His assault on the automobile clearly had me worried. Living in grey England, what I most treasured of my Shanghai childhood were my memories of American cars, a passion I've retained to this day. Looking back, one can see that Nader was the first of the eco-puritans, who proliferate now, convinced that everything is bad for us.

In fact, too few things are bad for us, and one fears an indefinite future of pious bourgeois certitudes. It's curious that these puritans strike such a chord – there is a deep underlying unease about the rate of social change, but little apparent change is actually taking place. Most superficial change belongs in the context of the word 'new', as applied to refrigerator or lawn-mower design. Real change is largely invisible, as befits this age of invisible technology – and people have embraced VCRs, fax machines, word processors without a thought, along with the new social habits that have sprung up around them. They have also accepted the unique vocabulary and grammar of late-20th-century life (whose psychology I have tried to describe in the present book), though most would deny it vehemently if asked.

## CHAPTER NINE

## YOU AND ME AND THE CONTINUUM

*The attempt to break into the Tomb of the Unknown Soldier on Good Friday, 197—, first assumed to be the act of some criminal psychopath, later led to inquiries of a very different character. Readers will recall that the little evidence collected seemed to point to the strange and confusing figure of an unidentified Air Force pilot whose body was washed ashore on a beach near Dieppe three months later. Other traces of his 'mortal remains' were found in a number of unexpected places: in a footnote to a paper on some unusual aspects of schizophrenia published thirty years earlier in a since defunct psychiatric journal; in the pilot for an unpurchased TV thriller, 'Lieutenant 70'; and on the record labels of a pop singer known as* The Him – *to instance only a few. Whether in fact this man was a returning astronaut suffering from amnesia, the figment of an ill-organized advertising campaign, or, as some have suggested, the second coming of Christ, is anyone's guess. What little evidence we have has been assembled below.*

**Ambivalent.** She lay quietly on her side, listening to the last bars of the scherzo as his hand hesitated on the zip. This strange man, and his endless obsession with Bruckner, nucleic acids, Minkowski space-time and God knows what else. Since meeting him at the conference on Space Medicine they had barely exchanged a word. Was he wholly there? At times it was almost as if he were trying to put himself together out of some bizarre jigsaw. She turned round, surprised by his dark glasses six inches from her face and the eyes burning through them like stars.

**Brachycephalic.** They stopped beneath the half-painted bowl of the radio-telescope. As the blunt metal ear turned on its tracks, fumbling at the sky, he put his hands to his skull, feeling the still-open sutures. Beside him Quinton, the dapper pomaded Judas, was waving at the distant hedges where the three limousines were waiting. 'If you like we can have a hundred cars – a complete motorcade.' Ignoring Quinton, he took a piece of quartz from his flying jacket and laid it on the turf. From it poured the code-music of the quasars.

**Coded Sleep.** Dr Nathan looked up as the young woman in the white coat entered the laboratory. 'Ah, Doctor Austin.' He pointed with his cigarette to the journal on his desk. 'This monograph – "Coded Sleep and Intertime" – they can't trace the author . . . someone at this Institute, apparently. I've assured them it's not a hoax. By the way, where's our volunteer?'

'He's asleep.' She hesitated, but only briefly. 'In my apartment.'

'So.' Before she left Dr Nathan said, 'Take a blood sample. His group may prove interesting at a later date.'

**Delivery System.** Certainly not an ass. Recent research, the lecturer pointed out, indicated that cosmic space vehicles may have been seen approaching the earth two thousand years earlier. As for the New Testament story, it had long been accepted that the unusual detail (Matt. XXI) of the Messiah riding into Jerusalem on 'an ass and a colt the foal of an ass' was an unintelligently literal reading of a tautological Hebrew idiom, a mere verbal blunder. 'What is space?' the lecturer concluded. 'What does it mean to our sense of time and the images we carry of our finite lives? Are space vehicles merely overgrown V-2s, or are they Jung's symbols of redemption, ciphers in some futuristic myth?'

As the applause echoed around the half-empty amphitheatre Karen Novotny saw his hands stiffen against the mirror on his lap. All week he had been bringing the giant mirrors to the empty house near the reservoirs.

**Export Credit Guarantees.** 'After all, Madame Nhu is asking a thousand dollars an interview, in this case we can insist on five and get it. Damn it, this is The Man . . .' The brain dulls. An exhibition of atrocity photographs rouses a flicker of interest. Meanwhile, the quasars burn dimly from the dark peaks of the universe. Standing across the room from Catherine Austin, who watches him with guarded eyes, he hears himself addressed as 'Paul', as if waiting for clandestine messages from the resistance headquarters of World War III.

**Five Hundred Feet High.** The Madonnas move across London like immense clouds. Painted on clapboard in the Mantegna style, their composed faces gaze down on the crowds watching from the streets below. Several hundred pass by, vanishing into the haze over the Queen Mary Reservoir, Staines, like a procession of marine deities. Some remarkable entrepreneur has arranged this tour de force; in advertising circles everyone is talking about the mysterious international agency that now has the Vatican account. At the Institute Dr Nathan is trying to sidestep the Late Renaissance. 'Mannerism bores me. Whatever happens,' he confides to Catherine Austin, 'we must keep him off Dali and Ernst.'

**Gioconda.** As the slides moved through the projector the women's photographs, in profile and full face, jerked one by one across the screen. 'A characteristic of the criminally insane,' Dr Nathan remarked, 'is the lack of tone and rigidity of the facial mask.'

The audience fell silent. An extraordinary woman had appeared on the screen. The planes of her face seemed to lead towards some invisible focus, projecting an image that lingered on the walls, as if they were inhabiting her skull. In her eyes glowed the forms of archangels. 'That one?' Dr Nathan asked quietly. 'Your mother? I see.'

**Helicopter.** The huge fans of the Sikorsky beat the air fifty feet above them as they drove into the town, a tornado of dust subsiding through the shattered trees along the road. Quinton sat back at the wheel of the Lincoln, now and then signalling over his shoulder at the helicopter pilot. As the music pounded from the radio of the car Quinton shouted, 'What a beat! Is this you as well? Now, what else do you need?' 'Mirrors, sand, a time shelter.'

**Imago Tapes.**
Tanguy: 'Jours de Lenteur.'
Ernst: 'The Robing of the Bride.'
de Chirico: 'The Dream of the Poet.'

**Jackie Kennedy, I See You in My Dreams.** At night the serene face of the President's widow hung like a lantern among the corridors of sleep. Warning him, she seemed

132

to summon to her side all the legions of the bereaved. At dawn he knelt in the grey hotel room over the copies of *Newsweek* and *Paris-Match*. When Karen Novotny called he borrowed her nail scissors and began to cut out the photographs of the model girls. 'In a dream I saw them lying on a beach. Their legs were rotting, giving out a green light.'

**Kodachrome.** Captain Webster studied the prints. They showed: (1) a thick-set man in an Air Force jacket, unshaven face half hidden by the dented hat-peak; (2) a transverse section through the spinal level T-12; (3) a crayon self-portrait by David Feary, seven-year-old schizophrenic at the Belmont Asylum, Sutton; (4) radio-spectra from the quasar CTA 102; (5) an antero-posterior radiograph of a skull, estimated capacity 1500 cc; (6) spectroheliogram of the sun taken with the K line of calcium; (7) left and right handprints showing massive scarring between second and third metacarpal bones. To Dr Nathan he said, 'And all these make up one picture?'

**Lieutenant 70.** An isolated incident at the Strategic Air Command base at Omaha, Nebraska, December 25th, 197—, when a landing H-bomber was found to have an extra pilot on board. The subject carried no identification tags and was apparently suffering from severe retrograde amnesia. He subsequently disappeared while being X-rayed at the base hospital for any bio-implants or transmitters, leaving behind a set of plates of a human foetus evidently taken some thirty years previously. It was assumed that this was in the nature of a hoax and that the subject was a junior officer who had become fatigued while playing Santa Claus on an inter-base visiting party.

**Minkowski Space-Time.** In part a confusion of mathematical models was responsible, Dr Nathan decided. Sitting behind his desk in the darkened laboratory, he drew slowly on the gold-tipped cigarette, watching the shadowy figure of a man seated opposite him, his back to the watery light from the aquarium tanks. At times part of his head seemed to be missing, like some disintegrating executive from a Francis Bacon nightmare. As yet irreconcilable data: his mother was a sixty-five-year-old terminal psychopath at Broadmoor, his father a still-unborn child in a Dallas lying-in hospital. Other fragments were beginning to appear in a variety of unlikely places: textbooks on chemical kinetics, advertising brochures, a pilot for a TV puppet thriller. Even the pun seemed to play a significant role, curious verbal crossovers. What language could embrace all these, or at least provide a key: computer codes, origami, dental formulae? Perhaps in the end Fellini would make a sex fantasy out of this botched second coming: 1½.

**Narcissistic.** Many things preoccupied him during this time in the sun: the plasticity of visual forms, the image maze, the need to re-score the central nervous system, pre-uterine claims, the absurd – i.e., the phenomenology of the universe ... The crowd at the plage, however, viewing this beach Hamlet, noticed only the scars which disfigured his chest, hands and feet.

**Ontologically Speaking.** In slow motion the test cars moved towards each other on collision courses, unwinding behind them the coils that ran to the metering devices by the impact zone. As they collided the gentle debris of wings and fenders floated into the air. The cars rocked slightly, worrying each other like amiable whales, and then continued on their disintegrating courses. In the passenger seats the plastic models transcribed graceful arcs into the buckling roofs and windshields. Here and there a passing fender severed a torso, the air behind the cars was a carnival of arms and legs.

**Placenta.** The X-ray plates of the growing foetus had shown the absence of both placenta and umbilical cord. Was this then, Dr Nathan pondered, the true meaning of the immaculate conception – that not the mother but the child was virgin, innocent of any Jocasta's clutching blood, sustained by the unseen powers of the universe as it lay waiting within its amnion? Yet why had something gone wrong? All too obviously there had been a complete cock-up.

**Quasars.** Malcolm X, beautiful as the trembling of hands in tabes dorsalis; Claude Eatherly, migrant angel of the Pre-Third; Lee Harvey Oswald, rider of the scorpion.

**Refuge.** Gripping the entrenching tool in his bloodied hands, he worked away at the lid of the vault. In the grey darkness of the Abbey the chips of cement seemed to draw light from his body. The bright crystals formed points like a half-familiar constellation, the crests of a volume graph, the fillings in Karen Novotny's teeth.

**Speed-King.** The highest speed ever achieved on land by a mechanically-propelled wheeled vehicle was 1004.247 m.p.h. reached at Bonneville Salt Flats on March 5th, 197—, by a twenty-seven-foot-long car powered by three J-79 aircraft engines developing a total of 51,000 h.p. The vehicle disintegrated at the end of the second run, and no trace was found of the driver, believed to be a retired Air Force pilot.

**The Him.**  The noise from the beat group rehearsing in the ballroom drummed at his head like a fist, driving away the half-formed equations that seemed to swim at him from the gilt mirrors in the corridor. What were they – fragments of a unified field theory, the tetragrammaton, or the production sequences for a deodorant pessary? Below the platform the party of teenagers the Savoy door-men had let in through the Embankment entrance were swaying to the music. He pushed through them to the platform. As he pulled the microphone away from the leader a girl jeered from the floor. Then his knees began to kick, his pelvis sliding and rocking. 'Ye . . . yeah, yeah, yeah!' he began, voice rising above the amplified guitars.

**U.H.F.**  'Considerable interference has been noted with TV reception over a wide area during the past three weeks,' Webster explained, pointing to the map. 'This has principally taken the form of modifications to the plot lines and narrative sequences of a number of family serials. Mobile detection vans have been unable to identify the source, but we may conclude that his central nervous system is acting as a powerful transmitter.'

**Vega.**  In the darkness the half-filled reservoirs reflected the starlight, the isolated heads of pumping gear marking the distant catwalks. Karen Novotny moved towards him, her white skirt lifted by the cold air. 'When do we see you again? This time, it's been . . .' He looked up at the night sky, then pointed to the blue star in the solar apex.

136

'Perhaps in time. We're moving there. Read the sand, it will tell you when.'

**W.A.S.P.** Without doubt there had been certain difficulties after the previous incarnation resulting from the choice of racial stock. Of course, from one point of view the unhappy events of our own century might be regarded as, say, demonstration ballets on the theme 'Hydrocarbon Synthesis' with strong audience participation. This time, however, no ethnic issues will be raised, and the needs for social mobility and a maximum acceptance personality profile make it essential that a subject of Gentile and preferably Protestant and Anglo-Saxon . . .

**Xoanon.** These small plastic puzzles, similar to the gew-gaws given away by petroleum and detergent manufac-turers, were found over a wide area, as if they had fallen from the sky. Millions had been produced, although their purpose was hard to see. Later it was found that unusual objects could be made from them.

**Ypres Reunion.** Webster waded through the breaking surf, following the tall man in the peaked cap and leather jacket who was moving slowly between the waves to the submerged sandbank two hundred yards away. Already pieces of the dying man were drifting past Webster in the water. Yet was this the time-man, or did his real remains lie in the tomb at the Abbey? He had come bearing the gifts of the sun and the quasars, and instead had sacrificed them for this unknown soldier resurrected now to return to his Flanders field.

**Zodiac.** Undisturbed, the universe would continue on its round, the unrequited ghosts of Malcolm X, Lee Harvey

Oswald and Claude Eatherly raised on the shoulders of the galaxy. As his own identity faded, its last fragments glimmered across the darkening landscape, lost integers in a hundred computer codes, sand-grains on a thousand beaches, fillings in a million mouths.

*Ambivalent.*

Throughout *The Atrocity Exhibition* its central character has appeared in a succession of roles, ranging across a spectrum of possibilities available to each of us in our interior lives. In the most abstract role, 'You: Coma: Marilyn Monroe', he behaves like an element in a geometric equation. In 'The Summer Cannibals' he is his most mundane and everyday self. Here, in 'You and Me and the Continuum', he is at his most apocalyptic, appearing as the second coming of Christ.

*Delivery System.*

Deserts possess a particular magic, since they have exhausted their own futures, and are thus free of time. Anything erected there, a city, a pyramid, a motel, stands outside time. It's no coincidence that religious leaders emerge from the desert. Modern shopping malls have much the same function. A future Rimbaud, Van Gogh or Adolf Hitler will emerge from their timeless wastes.

Some of the best American thrillers have been set in the desert – *The Getaway, The Hitcher, Charley Varrick, Blood Simple.* Given that there is no time past and no future, the idea of death and retribution has a doubly threatening force.

*Five Hundred Feet High.*

The reservoirs. Shepperton, noted for its film studios, lies on the River Thames some 15 miles to the west of London. All around are the high embankments of huge water reservoirs. Their contents remain completely hidden, until one flies into Heathrow Airport. It always surprises me to see that I live on the floor of an immense marine landscape.

The same sense of a concealed marine world occurs when I drive up into the hills above the French Riviera. Leaving behind the coastal strip of marinas and autoroutes, one seems to enter the Provence of a hundred years ago, a Cézanne country of secluded villas with terra-cotta roofs. Then, from an observation post high above Grasse, there is the astounding sight of scores of blue rectangles cut into the mountain sides – swimming pools. 100,000 years from now, when the human race has vanished, visitors from the stars will observe these drained concrete pits, many decorated with tritons and solar emblems. What were they – submerged marine altars? All that is left of the time-machines which these people used to escape from their planet? Three-dimensional symbols in a ritual geometry, models of a state of mind, votive offerings to the distant sea? One has the same impression flying over Beverly Hills.

*Imago Tapes.*
In 1966, when I wrote this chapter, the surrealists had not yet achieved critical respectability, but the hidden logic of that decade made complete sense in terms of their work. Readers will have noticed that, by contrast, there are almost no references to literary works. The realist novel still dominant then had exhausted itself.

*Lieutenant 70.*
During the Apollo flights I half-hoped that one of the spacecraft would return with an extra crew-man on board, wholly accepted by the others, who would shield him from a prying world. Watching the astronauts being interviewed together, one almost senses that they constitute a secret fraternity, and may be guarding some vital insight into the nature of time and space which it would be pointless to reveal to the rest of us. Unless the space programme resumes, the secret may die with them.

*Quasars.*

Claude Eatherly was the pilot of the reconnaissance B-29 which flew ahead of the Enola Gay during the A-bomb attack on Hiroshima. Eatherly had an unhappy later career, plagued by mental trouble and petty crime, which he attributed to his feelings of guilt. My guess is that he recognized, unconsciously or not, the public's need in the 1950s for someone who would incarnate their own sense of unease, and deflect their even greater fears of the H-bomb.

*Speed-King.*

Describing the Bonneville Salt Flats in *America*, Jean Baudrillard remarks that the extreme horizontality of the landscape, flatter than anywhere else on earth, demanded the high-speed record attempts as a means of neutralizing that horizontality.

*The Him.*

There is a British pop group called *God*. At a recent book signing the lead singer introduced himself and gave me a cassette. I have heard the voice of God.

*Vega.*

Our galaxy is moving in the direction of the constellation Vega. Given that time dilation occurs, not only when we travel through space, but when we think about space, the rendezvous may be sooner than we expect.

## CHAPTER TEN

# PLAN FOR THE ASSASSINATION OF JACQUELINE KENNEDY

**In his dream of Zapruder frame 235**

Motion picture studies of four female subjects who have achieved worldwide celebrity (Brigitte Bardot, Jacqueline Kennedy, Madame Chiang Kai-Shek, Princess Margaret), reveal common patterns of posture, facial tonus, pupil and respiratory responses. Leg stance was taken as a significant indicator of sexual arousal. The intra-patellar distance (estimated) varied from a maximum 24.9 cm (Jacqueline Kennedy) to a minimum 2.2 cm (Madame Chiang). Infrared studies reveal conspicuous heat emission from the axillary fossae at rates which tallied with general psychomotor acceleration.

**Tallis was increasingly preoccupied**

Assassination fantasies in tabes dorsalis (general paralysis of the insane). The choice of victim in these fantasies was taken as the most significant yardstick. All considerations of motive and responsibility were eliminated from the questionnaire. The patients were deliberately restricted in their choice to female victims. Results (percentile of 272 patients): Jacqueline Kennedy 62 percent, Madame Chiang 14 percent, Jeanne Moreau 13 percent, Princess Margaret 11 percent. A montage photograph was constructed on the basis of these replies which showed an 'optimum' victim. (Left orbit and zygomatic arch of Mrs Kennedy, exposed nasal septum of Miss Moreau, etc.) This photograph was subsequently shown to disturbed children with positive results. Choice of assassination site varied from Dealey Plaza 49 percent to Isle du Levant 2 percent. The weapon of preference was the Mannlicher-Carcano. A motorcade was selected in the overwhelming majority of cases as the ideal target mode with the Lincoln Continental as the vehicle of preference. On the basis of these studies a model of the most effective assassination-complex was devised. The presence of Madame Chiang in Dealey Plaza was an unresolved element.

### by the figure of the President's wife.

Involuntary orgasms during the cleaning of automobiles. Studies reveal an increasing incidence of sexual climaxes among persons cleaning automobiles. In many cases the subject remained unaware of the discharge of semen across the polished paintwork and complained to his spouse about birds. One isolated case reported to a psychiatric after-care unit involved the first definitive sexual congress with a rear exhaust assembly. It is believed that the act was conscious. Consultations with manufacturers have led to modifications of rear trim and styling, in order to neutralize these erogenous zones, or if possible transfer them to more socially acceptable areas within the passenger compartment. The steering assembly has been selected as a suitable focus for sexual arousal.

### The planes of her face, like the

The arousal potential of automobile styling has been widely examined for several decades by the automotive industry. However, in the study under consideration involving 152 subjects, all known to have experienced more than three involuntary orgasms with their automobiles, the car of preference was found to be (1) Buick Riviera, (2) Chrysler Imperial, (3) Chevrolet Impala. However, a small minority (2 subjects) expressed a significant preference for the Lincoln Continental, if possible in the adapted Presidential version (qv conspiracy theories). Both subjects had purchased cars of this make and experienced continuing erotic fantasies in connection with the trunk mouldings. Both preferred the automobile inclined on a downward ramp.

**cars of the abandoned motorcade**

Cine-films as group therapy. Patients were encouraged to form a film production unit, and were given full freedom as to choice of subject matter, cast and technique. In all cases explicitly pornographic films were made. Two films in particular were examined: (1) A montage sequence using portions of the faces of (a) Madame Ky, (b) Jeanne Moreau, (c) Jacqueline Kennedy (Johnson oath-taking). The use of a concealed stroboscopic device produced a major optical flutter in the audience, culminating in psychomotor disturbances and aggressive attacks directed against the still photographs of the subjects hung from the walls of the theatre. (2) A film of automobile accidents devised as a cinematic version of Nader's *Unsafe at Any Speed*. By chance it was found that slow-motion sequences of this film had a marked sedative effect, reducing blood pressure, respiration and pulse rates. Hypnagogic images were produced freely by patients. The film was also found to have a marked erotic content.

**mediated to him the complete silence**

Mouth-parts. In the first study, portions were removed from photographs of three well-known figures: Madame Chiang, Elizabeth Taylor, Jacqueline Kennedy. Patients were asked to fill in the missing areas. Mouth-parts provided a particular focus for aggression, sexual fantasies and retributive fears. In a subsequent test the original portion containing the mouth was replaced and the remainder of the face removed. Again particular attention was focused on the mouth-parts. Images of the mouth-parts of Madame Chiang and Jacqueline Kennedy had a notable hypotensive role. An optimum mouth-image of Madame Chiang and Mrs Kennedy was constructed.

**of the plaza, the geometry of a murder.**

Sexual behaviour of witnesses in Dealey Plaza. Detailed studies were conducted of the 552 witnesses in Dealey Plaza on November 22nd (Warren Report). Data indicate a significant upswing in (a) frequency of sexual intercourse, (b) incidence of polyperverse behaviour. These results accord with earlier studies of the sexual behaviour of spectators at major automobile accidents (=minimum of one death). Correspondences between the two groups studied indicate that for the majority of the spectators the events in Dealey Plaza were unconsciously perceived as those of a massive multiple-sex auto-disaster, with consequent liberation of aggressive and polymorphously perverse drives. The role of Mrs Kennedy, and of her stained clothing, requires no further analysis.

*'But I won't cry till it's all over.'*

*Plan for the Assassination of Jacqueline Kennedy*

The media landscape of the present day is a map in search of a territory. A huge volume of sensational and often toxic imagery inundates our minds, much of it fictional in content. How do we make sense of this ceaseless flow of advertising and publicity, news and entertainment, where presidential campaigns and moon voyages are presented in terms indistinguishable from the launch of a new candy bar or deodorant? What actually happens on the level of our unconscious minds when, within minutes on the same TV screen, a prime minister is assassinated, an actress makes love, an injured child is carried from a car crash? Faced with these charged events, prepackaged emotions already in place, we can only stitch together a set of emergency scenarios, just as our sleeping minds extemporize a narrative from the unrelated memories that veer through the cortical night. In the waking dream that now constitutes everyday reality, images of a blood-spattered widow, the chromium trim of a limousine windshield, the stylized glamour of a motorcade, fuse together to provide a secondary narrative with very different meanings.

'Plan for the Assassination of Jacqueline Kennedy' was written in 1967 and published in *Ambit*, the literary magazine edited by Dr Martin Bax. Somehow it came to the attention of Randolph Churchill (son of Winston), a former Member of Parliament and friend of the Kennedys. He denounced the piece, calling it an outrageous slur on the memory of the dead President, and demanded that the Arts Council withdraw its grant.

Soon after we were in trouble again, when *Ambit* launched a competition for the best fiction or poetry written under the influence of drugs. Lord Goodman, an intimate of Prime Minister Harold Wilson, raised the threat of prosecution. In fact, we were equally interested in the effects of legal drugs – tranquillizers, antihistamines, even baby aspirin. The competition, and the 40-pound prize which I offered, was won by the novelist Ann Quin – her drug was the oral contraceptive. She herself was a tragic figure, a beautiful but withdrawn woman who might have strayed from the pages of *The Atrocity Exhibition*. As her schizophrenia deepened she embarked on a series of impulsive journeys all over Europe, analogues perhaps of some mysterious movement within her mind. Eventually she walked into the sea off the south coast of England and drowned herself.

## CHAPTER ELEVEN

## LOVE AND NAPALM: EXPORT U.S.A.

**At night, these visions of helicopters and the D.M.Z.**

Sexual stimulation by newsreel atrocity films. Studies were conducted to determine the effects of long-term exposure to TV newsreel films depicting the torture of Viet Cong: (a) male combatants, (b) women auxiliaries, (c) children, (d) wounded. In all cases a marked increase in the intensity of sexual activity was reported, with particular emphasis on perverse oral and ano-genital modes. Maximum arousal was provided by combined torture and execution sequences. Montage newsreels were constructed in which leading public figures associated with the Vietnam war, e.g. President Johnson, General Westmoreland, Marshal Ky, were substituted for both combatants and victims. On the basis of viewers' preferences an optimum torture and execution sequence was devised involving Governor Reagan, Madame Ky and an unidentifiable eight-year-old Vietnamese girl napalm victim. Paedophiliac fantasies of a strongly sadistic character, i.e. involving repeated genital penetration of perineal wounds, were particularly stimulated by the child victim. Prolonged exposure to the film was found to have notable effects on all psychomotor activity. The film was subsequently shown to both disturbed children and terminal cancer patients with useful results.

**fused in Traven's mind with the spectre**

Combat films and the clinically insane. Endless-loop newsreels of Vietnam combat were shown to (a) an audience research panel, (b) psychotic patients (tertiary syphilis). In both cases combat films, as opposed to torture and execution sequences, were found to have a marked hypotensive role, regulating blood pressure, pulse and respiratory rates to acceptable levels. These results accord with the low elements of drama and interest in routine combat newsreels. However, by intercutting this psycho-physiological Muzak with atrocity films it was found that an optimum environment was created in which work-tasks, social relationships and overall motivation reached sustained levels of excellence. Given present socio-economic conditions, the advisability of maintaining the Vietnam war seems self-evident. Substitute military or civil conflicts, e.g. the imminent black–white race war, have proved disappointing in preliminary surveys, and the overall preference is thus for wars of the Vietnam type.

**of his daughter's body. The lantern of her face**

Vietnam and sexual polymorphism of individualized relationships of a physical character. The need for more polymorphic roles has been demonstrated by television and news media. Sexual intercourse can no longer be regarded as a personal and isolated activity, but is seen to be a vector in a public complex involving automobile styling, politics and mass communications. The Vietnam war has offered a focus for a wide range of polymorphic sexual impulses, and also a means by which the United States has re-established a positive psychosexual relationship with the external world.

148

**hung among the corridors of sleep.**

Tests were carried out to assess the sexual desirability of various national and ethnic groups. Montage photographs were constructed in which various features, e.g. face of Madame Chiang, pudenda of Viet Cong women prisoners, were selected to create the optimum sexual object. In all cases a marked preference was shown for a Vietnamese partner. Disguised elements depicting the faces of wounded children suffering severe facial pain were repeatedly chosen by panels of students, suburban housewives and psychotic patients. Further studies are in progress to construct an optimum sexual module involving mass merchandizing, atrocity newsreels and political figures. The key role of the Vietnam war is positively indicated throughout.

**Warning him, she summoned to her side**

The latent sexual character of the war. All political and military explanations fail to provide a rationale for the war's extended duration. In its manifest phase the war can be seen as a limited military confrontation with strong audience participation via TV and news media, satisfying low-threshold fantasies of violence and aggression. Tests confirm that the war has also served a latent role of strongly polymorphic character. Endless-loop combat and atrocity newsreels were intercut with material of genital, axillary, buccal and anal character. The expressed faecal matter of execution sequences was found to have a particular fascination for middle-income housewives. Prolonged exposure to these films may exercise a beneficial effect on the toilet training and psychosexual development of the present infant generation.

**all the legions of the bereaved.**

The effectiveness of a number of political figures, e.g. Governor Reagan and Shirley Temple, in mediating the latent sexual elements of the war indicates that this may well be their primary role. Montage photographs demonstrate the success of (a) the late President Kennedy in mediating a genital modulus of the war, and (b) Governor Reagan and Mrs Temple Black in mediating an anal modulus. Further tests were devised to assess the latent sexual fantasies of anti-war demonstrators. These confirm the hysterical nature of reactions to films of napalm victims and A.R.V.N. atrocities, and indicate that for the majority of so-called peace groups the Vietnam war serves the role of masking repressed sexual inadequacies of an extreme nature.

## By day the overflights of B-52s

Psychotic patients exposed to continuous Vietnam war newsreel material have shown marked improvements in overall health, self-maintenance and ability to cope with tasks. Similar advances have been shown by disturbed children. Deprivation of newsreel and TV screenings led to symptoms of withdrawal and a lowering of general health. This accords with the behaviour of a volunteer group of suburban housewives during New Year truce periods. Levels of overall health and sexual activity fell notably, only restored by the Tet offensive and the capture of the U.S. embassy. Suggestions have been made for increasing the violence and latent sexuality of the war, and current peace moves may require the manufacture of simulated newsreels. Already it has been shown that simulated films of the execution and maltreatment of children have notably beneficial effects on the awareness and verbal facility of psychotic children.

150

**crossed the drowned causeways of the delta,**

Fake atrocity films. Comparison of Vietnam atrocity films with fake newsreels of Auschwitz, Belsen and the Congo reveals that the Vietnam war far exceeds the latter's appeal and curative benefits. As part of their therapy programme a group of patients were encouraged to devise a fake atrocity film employing photographs of buccal, rectal and genital mutilations intercut with images of political figures.

**unique ciphers of violence and desire.**

Optimum child-mutilation film. Using assembly kits of atrocity photographs, groups of housewives, students and psychotic patients selected the optimum child-torture victim. Rape and napalm burns remained constant preoccupations, and a wound profile of maximum arousal was constructed. Despite the revulsion expressed by the panels, follow-up surveys of work-proficiency and health patterns indicate substantial benefits. The effects of atrocity films on disturbed children were found to have positive results that indicate similar benefits for the TV public at large. These studies confirm that it is only in terms of a psychosexual module such as provided by the Vietnam war that the United States can enter into a relationship with the world generally characterized by the term 'love'.

*Love and Napalm: Export U.S.A.*
'Love and Napalm: Export U.S.A.' was the title chosen, against my advice, for the edition of *The Atrocity Exhibition* which Grove Press published in 1972. I remember sitting in a London hotel with Fred Jordan, the intelligent and likeable editor at Grove, and arguing against the title on the grounds (a) that the Vietnam war was over (this was 1971), and (b) that it would give an apparently anti-American slant to the whole

book. Jordan maintained that the war was not over and would continue to rouse violent passions for years to come. I felt that he was wrong, and that though the tragedy would cast its shadow for decades across America, the era of street protests and marches was over. Even from our side of the Atlantic it was clear that the U.S. public had seen more than enough of the war.

As for the apparent anti-Americanism, the hidden logic at work within the mass media – above all, the inadvertent packaging of violence and cruelty like attractive commercial products – had already spread throughout the world. If anything, the process was even more advanced in Britain. The equivalent of the U.S. television commercial on British TV is the 'serious' documentary, the ostensibly highminded 'news' programme that gives a seductive authority to the manipulated images of violence and suffering offered by the conscience-stricken presenters – an even more insidious form of pornography. Recognizing this, our new puritan watchdogs have recently called for censorship of the news. Corpses should never be shown at the scene, say, of an air crash, which gags our emotional response (and civic sense that something should be done), and may even engender the unconscious belief that a plane crash is an exciting event not far removed from a demolition derby. 'Responsible' TV is far more dangerous than the most mindless entertainment. At its worst, American TV merely trivializes the already trivial, while British TV consistently trivializes the serious.

## CHAPTER TWELVE

# CRASH!

### Each afternoon in the deserted cinema

The latent sexual content of the automobile crash. Numerous studies have been conducted to assess the latent sexual appeal of public figures who have achieved subsequent notoriety as auto-crash fatalities, e.g. James Dean, Jayne Mansfield, Albert Camus. Simulated newsreels of politicians, film stars and TV celebrities were shown to panels of (a) suburban housewives, (b) terminal paretics, (c) filling station personnel. Sequences showing auto-crash victims brought about a marked acceleration of pulse and respiratory rates. Many volunteers became convinced that the fatalities were still living, and later used one or other of the crash victims as a private focus of arousal during intercourse with the domestic partner.

### Tallis was increasingly distressed

Relatives of auto-crash victims showed a similar upsurge in both sexual activity and overall levels of general health. Mourning periods were drastically reduced. After a brief initial period of withdrawal, relatives would revisit the site, usually attempting a discreet re-enactment of the crash mode. In an extreme 2 percent of cases spontaneous orgasms were experienced during a simulated run along the crash route. Surprisingly, these results parallel the increased frequency of sexual intercourse in new-car families, the showroom providing a widely popular erotic focus. Incidence of neurosis in new-car families is also markedly less.

### by the images of colliding motor cars.

Behaviour of spectators at automobile accidents. The sexual behaviour of spectators at major automobile accidents (=minimum one death) has also been examined. In all cases there was a conspicuous improvement in both marital and extra-marital relationships, combined with a more tolerant attitude towards perverse behaviour. The 552 spectators of the Kennedy assassination in Dealey Plaza were observed closely in follow-up surveys. Overall health and frequency of sexual activity increased notably over subjects in nearby Elm and Commerce Streets. Police reports indicate that Dealey Plaza has since become a minor sexual nuisance area.

### Celebrations of his wife's death,

Pudenda of auto-crash victims. Using assembly kits constructed from photographs of (a) unidentified bodies of accident victims, (b) Cadillac exhaust assemblies, (c) the mouth-parts of Jacqueline Kennedy, volunteers were asked to devise the optimum auto-crash victim. The notional pudenda of crash victims exercised a particular fascination. Choice of subjects was as follows: 75 percent J. F. Kennedy, 15 percent James Dean, 9 percent Jayne Mansfield, 1 percent Albert Camus. In an open category test, volunteers were asked to name those living public figures most suitable as potential crash victims. Choices varied from Brigitte Bardot and Prof. Barnard to Mrs Pat Nixon and Madame Chiang.

**the slow-motion newsreels**

The optimum auto-disaster. Panels consisting of drive-in theatre personnel, students and middle-income housewives were encouraged to devise the optimum auto-disaster. A wide choice of impact modes was available, including roll-over, roll-over followed by head-on collision, multiple pile-ups and motorcade attacks. The choice of death-postures included (1) normal driving position, (2) sleep, rear seat, (3) acts of intercourse, by both driver and passenger, (4) severe anginal spasm. In an overwhelming majority of cases a crash complex was constructed containing elements not usually present in automobile accidents, i.e. strong religious and sexual overtones, the victim being mounted in the automobile in bizarre positions containing postural elements of both perverse intercourse and ritual sacrifice, e.g. arms outstretched in a notional crucifixion mode.

**recapitulated all his memories of childhood,**

The optimum wound profile. As part of a continuing therapy programme, patients devised the optimum wound profile. A wide variety of wounds was imagined. Psychotic patients showed a preference for facial and neck wounds. Students and filling station personnel overwhelmingly selected abdominal injuries. By contrast suburban house-wives expressed a marked preoccupation with severe gen-ital wounds of an obscene character. The accident modes which rationalized these choices reflected polyperverse obsessions of an extreme form.

**the realization of dreams**

The conceptual auto-disaster. The volunteer panels were shown fake safety propaganda movies in which implausible accidents were staged. Far from eliciting a humorous or sardonic response from the audience, marked feelings of hostility were shown towards the film and medical support staff. Subsequent films of genuine accidents exerted a notably calming effect. From this and similar work it is clear that Freud's classic distinction between the manifest and latent content of the inner world of the psyche now has to be applied to the outer world of reality. A dominant element in this reality is technology and its instrument, the machine. In most roles the machine assumes a benign or passive posture – telephone exchanges, engineering hardware, etc. The twentieth century has also given birth to a vast range of machines – computers, pilotless planes, thermonuclear weapons – where the latent identity of the machine is ambiguous even to the skilled investigator. An understanding of this identity can be found in a study of the automobile, which dominates the vectors of speed, aggression, violence and desire. In particular the automobile crash contains a crucial image of the machine as conceptualized psychopathology. Tests on a wide range of subjects indicate that the automobile, and in particular the automobile crash, provides a focus for the conceptualizing of a wide range of impulses involving the elements of psychopathology, sexuality and self-sacrifice.

**which even during the safe immobility of sleep**

Preferred death modes. Subjects were given a choice of various death modes and asked to select those they would most fear for themselves and their families. Suicide and murder proved without exception to be most feared, followed by air disasters, domestic electrocution and drowning. Death by automobile accident was uniformly considered to be least objectionable, in spite of the often extended death ordeal and severe mutilatory injuries.

**would develop into nightmares of anxiety.**

Psychology of crash victims. Studies have been carried out on the recuperative behaviour of crash victims. The great majority of cases were aided by any opportunity of unconscious identification with such fatalities as J. F. Kennedy, Jayne Mansfield and James Dean. Although many patients continued to express a strong sense of anatomical loss (an extreme 2 percent of cases maintained against all evidence that they had lost their genitalia) this was not regarded as any form of deprivation. It is clear that the car crash is seen as a fertilizing rather than a destructive experience, a liberation of sexual and machine libido, mediating the sexuality of those who have died with an erotic intensity impossible in any other form.

*Crash!*
This 1968 piece was written a year before my exhibition of crashed cars at the New Arts Laboratory, and in effect is the gene from which my novel *Crash* was to spring. The ambiguous role of the car crash needs no elaboration – apart from our own deaths, the car crash is probably the most dramatic event in our lives, and in many cases the two will coincide. Aside from the fact that we generally own or are at the controls of the crashing vehicle, the car crash differs from other disasters in that it involves the most powerfully advertised commercial product of this century, an iconic entity that combines the elements of speed, power, dream and freedom within a highly stylised format that defuses any fears we may have of the inherent dangers of these violent and unstable machines.

Americans are now scarcely aware of automobile styling, but the subject has always intrigued me, and seems a remarkably accurate barometer of national confidence. When I visited the U.S.A. in 1955 all the optimism of Eisenhower's post-war America was expressed in the baroque vehicles that soared along its highways, as if an advanced interstellar race had touched down on a recreational visit. But the doubts engendered by the Soviet H-bomb, the death of Kennedy and the Vietnam war led to a slab-sided and unornamented flatness, culminating in the Mercedes look, simultaneously aggressive and defensive, like German medieval armour, among the most dark and paranoid I have ever seen. On my last visit to the States, in 1988, I was happy to see that 1950s exuberance was returning.

I take it for granted, by the way, that only American cars are truly *styled*. European cars are merely streamlined, though within those limits, as in the Delahaye, Lagonda and Jaguar, there have appeared some of the most beautiful objects ever made, a reminder of Marinetti's dictum that 'a racing car is more beautiful than the Winged Victory of Samothrace'. For those interested, she stands arms outstretched in the lobby of the Louvre, and the contest is a close-run thing, much as I admire Marinetti and the futurists. But only the most advanced Italian concept cars break free of streamlining into a strange, interiorized realm of their own, where their complex body shells seem to be trying to escape from time and space altogether. The ultimate concept car will move so fast, even at rest, as to be invisible.

## CHAPTER THIRTEEN

# THE GENERATIONS OF AMERICA

**These are the generations of America.**

Sirhan Sirhan shot Robert F. Kennedy. And Ethel M. Kennedy shot Judith Birnbaum. And Judith Birnbaum shot Elizabeth Bochnak. And Elizabeth Bochnak shot Andrew Witwer. And Andrew Witwer shot John Burlingham. And John Burlingham shot Edward R. Darlington. And Edward R. Darlington shot Valerie Gerry. And Valerie Gerry shot Olga Giddy. And Olga Giddy shot Rita Goldstein. And Rita Goldstein shot Bob Monterola. And Bob Monterola shot Barbara H. Nicolosi. And Barbara H. Nicolosi shot Geraldine Carro. And Geraldine Carro shot Jeanne Voltz. And Jeanne Voltz shot Joseph P. Steiner. And Joseph P. Steiner shot Donald Van Dyke. And Donald Van Dyke shot Anne M. Schumacher. And Anne M. Schumacher shot Ralph K. Smith. And Ralph K. Smith shot Laurence J. Whitmore. And Laurence J. Whitmore shot Virginia B. Adams. And Virginia B. Adams shot Lynn Young. And Lynn Young shot Lucille Beachy. And Lucille Beachy shot John J. Concannon. And John J. Concannon shot Ainslie Dinwiddie. And Ainslie Dinwiddie shot Dianne Zimmerman. And Dianne Zimmerman shot Gerson Zelman. And Gerson Zelman shot Paula C. Dubroff. And Paula C. Dubroff shot Ebbe Ebbeson. And Ebbe Ebbeson shot Constance Wiley. And Constance Wiley shot Milton Unger. And Milton Unger shot Kenneth Sarvis.

And Kenneth Sarvis shot Ruth Ross. And Ruth Ross shot August Muggenthaler. And August Muggenthaler shot Phyllis Malamud. And Phyllis Malamud shot Josh Eppinger III. And Josh Eppinger III shot Kermit Lanser. And Kermit Lanser shot Lester Bernstein. And Lester Bernstein shot Frank Trippett. And Frank Trippett shot Wade Greene. And Wade Greene shot Kenneth Auchincloss. And Kenneth Auchincloss shot Bruce Porter. And Bruce Porter shot John Lake. And John Lake shot John Mitchell. And John Mitchell shot Kenneth L. Woodward. And Kenneth L. Woodward shot Lee Smith. And Lee Smith shot Arthur Cooper. And Arthur Cooper shot Arthur Higbee. And Arthur Higbee shot Anne M. Schlesinger. And Anne M. Schlesinger shot Jonathan B. Peel. And Jonathan B. Peel shot Ruth Wertham. And Ruth Wertham shot David L. Shirey. And David L. Shirey shot Saul Melvin. And Saul Melvin shot Penelope Eakins. And Penelope Eakins shot Mary K. Doris. And Mary K. Doris shot Melvyn Gussow. And Melvyn Gussow shot Roger De Borger. And Roger De Borger shot Edward Cumberbatch. And Edward Cumberbatch shot Shirlee Hoffman. And Shirlee Hoffman shot Jayne Brumley. And Jayne Brumley shot Joel Blocker. And Joel Blocker shot George Gaal. And George Gaal shot Ted Slate. And Ted Slate shot Mary B. Hood. And Mary B. Hood shot Laurence S. Martz. And Laurence S. Martz shot Harry F. Waters. And Harry F. Waters shot Archer Speers. And Archer Speers shot Kelvin P. Buckley. And Kelvin P. Buckley shot George Fitzgerald. And George Fitzgerald shot Lew L. Callaway. And Lew L. Callaway shot Gibson McCabe. And Gibson McCabe shot Americo Calvo. And Americo Calvo shot Francois Sully. And Francois Sully shot Edward Klein. And Edward Klein shot Edward Weintal. And Edward Weintal shot Arleigh

Burke. And Arleigh Burke shot James C. Thompson. And James C. Thompson shot Alison Knowles. And Alison Knowles shot Walter Hinchup. And Walter Hinchup shot Pedlar Forrest. And Pedlar Forrest shot Jim Gym. And Jim Gym shot James McBride. And James McBride shot Cyrus Partovi. And Cyrus Partovi shot Lewis P. Bohler.

And James Earl Ray shot Martin Luther King. And Coretta King shot Jacqueline Fisher. And Jacqueline Fisher shot Ernest Brennecke. And Ernest Brennecke shot Peggy Bomba. And Peggy Bomba shot Barry A. Erlich. And Barry A. Erlich shot James E. Huddleston. And James E. Huddleston shot Jerry Miller. And Jerry Miller shot Robert Nordvall. And Robert Nordvall shot William E. Harris. And William E. Harris shot Marguerite Sekots. And Marguerite Sekots shot Vernard Foley. And Vernard Foley shot Dale C. Kisteler. And Dale C. Kisteler shot Bruce Sperber. And Bruce Sperber shot Kay Flaherty. And Kay Flaherty shot Sol Babitz. And Sol Babitz shot Richard M. Clurman. And Richard M. Clurman shot Frederick Gruin. And Frederic Gruin shot Edward Jackson. And Edward Jackson shot Judson Gooding. And Judson Gooding shot Rosemarie Zadikov. And Rosemarie Zadikov shot Donald Neff. And Donald Neff shot Joseph J. Kane. And Joseph J. Kane shot Mark Sullivan. And Mark Sullivan shot Barry Hillenbrand. And Barry Hillenbrand shot Linda Young. And Linda Young shot Nina Wilson. And Nina Wilson shot Jack Meyes. And Jack Meyes shot Arlie W. Schardt. And Arlie W. Schardt shot Roger M. Williams. And Roger M. Williams shot Marcia Gauger. And Marcia Gauger shot Nancy Williams. And Nancy Williams shot Susanne W. Washburn. And Susanne W. Washburn shot Timothy Tyler. And Timothy Tyler shot David C. Lee. And David C. Lee shot

James E. Broadhead. And James E. Broadhead shot Robert S. Anson. And Robert S. Anson shot Robert Parker. And Robert Parker shot Donald Birmingham. And Donald Birmingham shot John Steele. And John Steele shot Fortunata Vanderschmidt. And Fortunata Vanderschmidt shot Stephanie Trimble. And Stephanie Trimble shot Hugh Sidey. And Hugh Sidey shot Edwin W. Goodpaster. And Edwin W. Goodpaster shot Bonnie Angelo. And Bonnie Angelo shot Walter Bennett. And Walter Bennett shot Martha Reingold. And Martha Reingold shot Lane Fortinberry. And Lane Fortinberry shot Jess Cook. And Jess Cook shot Kenneth Danforth. And Kenneth Danforth shot Marshall Berges. And Marshall Berges shot Samuel R. Iker. And Samuel R. Iker shot John F. Stacks. And John F. Stacks shot Paul R. Hathaway. And Paul R. Hathaway shot Raissa Silverman. And Raissa Silverman shot Patricia Gordon. And Patricia Gordon shot Greta Davis. And Greta Davis shot Harriet Bachman. And Harriet Bachman shot Charles B. Wheat. And Charles B. Wheat shot William Bender. And William Bender shot Alan Washburn. And Alan Washburn shot Julie Adams. And Julie Adams shot Susan Saner. And Susan Saner shot Richard Burgheim. And Richard Burgheim shot Larry Still. And Larry Still shot Alten L. Clingen. And Alten L. Clingen shot Jerry Kirshenbaum.

And Lee Harvey Oswald shot John F. Kennedy. And Jacqueline Kennedy shot Mark S. Goodman. And Mark S. Goodman shot Beverley Davis. And Beverley Davis shot James Willwerth. And James Willwerth shot John J. Austin. And John J. Austin shot Nancy Jalet. And Nancy Jalet shot Leah Shanks. And Leah Shanks shot Christopher Porterfield. And Christopher Porterfield shot Edward Hughes. And Edward Hughes shot Madeleine Berry. And

Madeleine Berry shot Hilary Newman. And Hilary Newman shot James A. Linen. And James A. Linen shot James Keogh. And James Keogh shot Putney Westerfield. And Putney Westerfield shot Oliver S. Moore. And Oliver S. Moore shot James Wilde. And James Wilde shot John T. Elson. And John T. Elson shot Rosemary Funger. And Rosemary Funger shot Piri Halasz. And Piri Halasz shot William Mader. And William Mader shot John Larsen. And John Larsen shot Joy Howden. And Joy Howden shot Andria Hourwich. And Andria Hourwich shot Betty Sukyer. And Betty Sukyer shot Ingrid Krosch. And Ingrid Krosch shot John Koffend. And John Koffend shot Rodney Sheppard. And Rodney Sheppard shot Ruth Brine. And Ruth Brine shot Judy Mitnick. And Judy Mitnick shot Paul Hathaway. And Paul Hathaway shot Manon Gaulin. And Manon Gaulin shot Katherine Prager. And Katherine Prager shot Marie Gibbons. And Marie Gibbons shot James E. Broadhead. And James E. Broadhead shot Philip Stacks. And Philip Stacks shot Peter Babcox. And Peter Babcox shot Christopher T. Cory. And Christopher T. Cory shot Erwin Edleman. And Erwin Edleman shot William Forbis. And William Forbis shot Ingrid Carroll.

These are the generations of America.

These names were taken from the editorial mastheads of *Look*, *Life* and *Time*, my only available source of large numbers of American surnames. The choice had nothing to do with the magazines themselves – I have been a keen reader of *Time* and *Life* since the late 1930s – though there is an unintended irony in recruiting the names from the editors and production staff of three mass-magazines that helped to create the media landscape at the heart of *The Atrocity Exhibition*.

Over the years, trying to get away from the provincially English surnames of the London phone book, I have taken a large number of my characters' names from the masthead of *Time*, though I never had the nerve to use the redoubtable Minnie Magazine. I soon noticed that Anglo-Saxon names seemed to rise effortlessly to the top of the mast, while Italian and Slavic names crowded the plinth. In recent years things have changed.

## CHAPTER FOURTEEN

# WHY I WANT TO FUCK RONALD REAGAN

## During these assassination fantasies

Ronald Reagan and the conceptual auto-disaster. Numerous studies have been conducted upon patients in terminal paresis (G.P.I.), placing Reagan in a series of simulated auto-crashes, e.g. multiple pile-ups, head-on collisions, motorcade attacks (fantasies of Presidential assassinations remained a continuing preoccupation, subjects showing a marked polymorphic fixation on windshields and rear trunk assemblies). Powerful erotic fantasies of an anal-sadistic character surrounded the image of the Presidential contender. Subjects were required to construct the optimum auto-disaster victim by placing a replica of Reagan's head on the unretouched photographs of crash fatalities. In 82 percent of cases massive rear-end collisions were selected with a preference for expressed faecal matter and rectal haemorrhages. Further tests were conducted to define the optimum model-year. These indicate that a three-year model lapse with child victims provide the maximum audience excitation (confirmed by manufacturers' studies of the optimum auto-disaster). It is hoped to construct a rectal modulus of Reagan and the auto-disaster of maximized audience arousal.

## Tallis became increasingly obsessed

Motion picture studies of Ronald Reagan reveal characteristic patterns of facial tonus and musculature associated with homo-erotic behaviour. The continuing tension of buccal sphincters and the recessive tongue role tally with earlier studies of facial rigidity (cf., Adolf Hitler, Nixon). Slow-motion cine-films of campaign speeches exercised a marked erotic effect upon an audience of spastic children. Even with mature adults the verbal material was found to have minimal effect, as demonstrated by substitution of an edited tape giving diametrically opposed opinions. Parallel films of rectal images revealed a sharp upsurge in anti-Semitic and concentration camp fantasies.

## with the pudenda of the Presidential contender

Incidence of orgasms in fantasies of sexual intercourse with Ronald Reagan. Patients were provided with assembly kit photographs of sexual partners during intercourse. In each case Reagan's face was superimposed upon the original partner. Vaginal intercourse with 'Reagan' proved uniformly disappointing, producing orgasm in 2 percent of subjects. Axillary, buccal, navel, aural and orbital modes produced proximal erections. The preferred mode of entry overwhelmingly proved to be the rectal. After a preliminary course in anatomy it was found that caecum and transverse colon also provided excellent sites for excitation. In an extreme 12 percent of cases, the simulated anus of post-colostomy surgery generated spontaneous orgasm in 98 percent of penetrations. Multiple-track cine-films were constructed of 'Reagan' in intercourse during (a) campaign speeches, (b) rear-end auto-collisions with one- and three-year-old model changes, (c) with rear-exhaust assemblies, (d) with Vietnamese child-atrocity victims.

**mediated to him by a thousand television screens.**

Sexual fantasies in connection with Ronald Reagan. The genitalia of the Presidential contender exercised a continuing fascination. A series of imaginary genitalia were constructed using (a) the mouth-parts of Jacqueline Kennedy, (b) a Cadillac rear-exhaust vent, (c) the assembly kit prepuce of President Johnson, (d) a child-victim of sexual assault. In 89 percent of cases, the constructed genitalia generated a high incidence of self-induced orgasm. Tests indicate the masturbatory nature of the Presidential contender's posture. Dolls consisting of plastic models of Reagan's alternate genitalia were found to have a disturbing effect on deprived children.

### The motion picture studies of Ronald Reagan

Reagan's hairstyle. Studies were conducted on the marked fascination exercised by the Presidential contender's hairstyle. 65 percent of male subjects made positive connections between the hairstyle and their own pubic hair. A series of optimum hairstyles were constructed.

### created a scenario of the conceptual orgasm,

The conceptual role of Reagan. Fragments of Reagan's cinetized postures were used in the construction of model psychodramas in which the Reagan-figure played the role of husband, doctor, insurance salesman, marriage counsellor, etc. The failure of these roles to express any meaning reveals the non-functional character of Reagan. Reagan's success therefore indicates society's periodic need to re-conceptualize its political leaders. Reagan thus appears as a series of posture concepts, basic equations which re-formulate the roles of aggression and anality.

167

**a unique ontology of violence and disaster.**

Reagan's personality. The profound anality of the Presidential contender may be expected to dominate the United States in the coming years. By contrast the late J. F. Kennedy remained the prototype of the oral object, usually conceived in pre-pubertal terms. In further studies sadistic psychopaths were given the task of devising sex fantasies involving Reagan. Results confirm the probability of Presidential figures being perceived primarily in genital terms; the face of L. B. Johnson is clearly genital in significant appearance – the nasal prepuce, scrotal jaw, etc. Faces were seen as either circumcized (JFK, Khrushchev) or uncircumcized (LBJ, Adenauer). In assembly kit tests Reagan's face was uniformly perceived as a penile erection. Patients were encouraged to devise the optimum sex-death of Ronald Reagan.

*Why I Want to Fuck Ronald Reagan.*
'Why I want to Fuck Ronald Reagan' prompted Doubleday in 1970 to pulp its first American edition of *The Atrocity Exhibition*. Ronald Reagan's presidency remained a complete mystery to most Europeans, though I noticed that Americans took him far more easily in their stride. But the amiable old duffer who occupied the White House was a very different person from the often sinister figure I described in 1967, when the present piece was first published. The then-novelty of a Hollywood film star entering politics and becoming governor of California gave Reagan considerable air-time on British TV. Watching his right-wing speeches, in which he castigated in sneering tones the profligate, welfare-spending, bureaucrat-infested state government, I saw a more crude and ambitious figure, far closer to the brutal crime boss he played in the 1964 movie, *The Killers*, his last Hollywood role. In his commercials Reagan used the smooth, teleprompter-perfect tones of the TV auto-salesman to project

a political message that was absolutely the reverse of bland and reassuring. A complete discontinuity existed between Reagan's manner and body language, on the one hand, and his scarily simplistic far-right message on the other. Above all, it struck me that Reagan was the first politician to exploit the fact that his TV audience would not be listening too closely, if at all, to what he was saying, and indeed might well assume from his manner and presentation that he was saying the exact opposite of the words actually emerging from his mouth. Though the man himself mellowed, his later presidency seems to have run to the same formula.

In 1968 the American poet Bill Butler, who ran the Unicorn Bookshop in Brighton on the south coast of England, published 'Why I Want to Fuck Ronald Reagan' as a separate booklet. Soon after, his bookshop, which specialized in European and American poetry and fiction, was raided by the police, and he was charged with selling obscene material – Burroughs and Bataille among others, if I remember, and my Reagan piece, which was selected as one of three offending exhibits brought to trial. A defence campaign was mounted, and I agreed to appear as a witness. Preparing me, the defence lawyer asked me why I believed 'Why I Want to Fuck Ronald Reagan' was not obscene, to which I had to reply that of course it was obscene, and intended to be so. Why, then, was its subject matter not Reagan's sexuality? Again I had to affirm that it was. At last the lawyer said: 'Mr Ballard, you will make a very good witness for the prosecution. We will not be calling you.'

The chief magistrate was a Brighton butcher appropriately named Mr Ripper. As expected, he humiliated the literary witnesses, ridiculing their evidence, and Bill Butler was found guilty. By chance the charge against the Reagan piece was dropped on the grounds that the envelope containing the seized copy was sealed. Sadly, all this led to a coolness between Bill and myself, which I was not able to repair before his death from a drug overdose some years later. I think he suspected me of over-deft footwork in side-stepping my obligations to him, but in fact he was in no danger of a prison sentence and I saw no reason to pretend that the Reagan piece was anything but a frontal assault on the former actor.

At the 1980 Republican Convention in San Francisco a copy of my Reagan text, minus its title and the running sideheads, and furnished with the seal of the Republican Party, was distributed to delegates. I'm told it was accepted for what it resembled, a psychological position paper on the candidate's subliminal appeal, commissioned from some maverick think-tank.

## CHAPTER FIFTEEN

# THE ASSASSINATION OF JOHN FITZGERALD KENNEDY CONSIDERED AS A DOWNHILL MOTOR RACE

**Author's Note.** *The assassination of President Kennedy on November 22, 1963, raised many questions, not all of which were answered by the Report of the Warren Commission. It is suggested that a less conventional view of the events of that grim day may provide a more satisfactory explanation. In particular, Alfred Jarry's 'The Crucifixion Considered as an Uphill Bicycle Race' gives us a useful lead.*

Oswald was the starter.

From his window above the track he opened the race by firing the starting gun. It is believed that the first shot was not properly heard by all the drivers. In the following confusion Oswald fired the gun two more times, but the race was already under way.

Kennedy got off to a bad start.

There was a governor in his car and its speed remained constant at about fifteen miles an hour. However, shortly afterwards, when the governor had been put out of action, the car accelerated rapidly, and continued at high speed along the remainder of the course.

The visiting teams. As befitting the inauguration of the first production car race through the streets of Dallas, both the President and the Vice-President participated. The Vice-President, Johnson, took up his position behind Kennedy on the starting line. The concealed rivalry between the two men was of keen interest to the crowd. Most of them supported the home driver, Johnson.

The starting point was the Texas Book Depository, where all bets were placed on the Presidential race. Kennedy was an unpopular contestant with the Dallas crowd, many of whom showed outright hostility. The deplorable incident familiar to us all is one example.

The course ran downhill from the Book Depository, below an overpass, then on to the Parkland Hospital and from there to Love Air Field. It is one of the most hazardous courses in downhill motor racing, second only to the Sarajevo track discontinued in 1914.

Kennedy went downhill rapidly. After the damage to the governor the car shot forward at high speed. An alarmed track official attempted to mount the car, which continued on its way, cornering on two wheels.

Turns. Kennedy was disqualified at the hospital, after taking a turn for the worse. Johnson now continued the race in the lead, which he maintained to the finish.

The flag. To signify the participation of the President in the race Old Glory was used in place of the usual chequered square. Photographs of Johnson receiving his prize after winning the race reveal that he had decided to make the flag a memento of his victory.

Previously, Johnson had been forced to take a back seat, as his position on the starting line behind the President indicates. Indeed, his attempts to gain a quick lead on Kennedy during the false start were forestalled by a track steward, who pushed Johnson to the floor of his car.

In view of the confusion at the start of the race, which resulted in Kennedy, clearly expected to be the winner on past form, being forced to drop out at the hospital turn, it has been suggested that the hostile local crowd, eager to see a win by the home driver Johnson, deliberately set out to stop him completing the race. Another theory maintains that the police guarding the track were in collusion with the starter, Oswald. After he finally managed to give the send-off Oswald immediately left the race, and was subsequently apprehended by track officials.

Johnson had certainly not expected to win the race in this way. There were no pit stops.

Several puzzling aspects of the race remain. One is the presence of the President's wife in the car, an unusual practice for racing drivers. Kennedy, however, may have maintained that as he was in control of the ship of state he was therefore entitled to captain's privileges.

The Warren Commission. The rake-off on the book of the race. In their report, prompted by widespread complaints of foul play and other irregularities, the syndicate lay full blame on the starter, Oswald.

Without doubt Oswald badly misfired. But one question still remains unanswered: who loaded the starting gun?

# APPENDIX

# PRINCESS MARGARET'S FACE LIFT

As Princess Margaret reached middle age, the skin of both her cheeks and neck tended to sag from failure of the supporting structures. Her naso-labial folds deepened, and the soft tissues along her jaw fell forward. Her jowls tended to increase. In profile the creases of her neck lengthened and the chin-neck contour lost its youthful outline and became convex.

The eminent plastic surgeon Richard Battle has remarked that one of the great misfortunes of the cosmetic surgeon is that he only has the technical skill, ability and understanding to correct this situation by surgical means. However, as long as people are prepared to pay fees for this treatment the necessary operation will be performed. Incisions made across the neck with the object of removing redundant tissue should be avoided. These scars tend to be unduly prominent and may prove to be the subject of litigation. In the case of Princess Margaret the incision was designed to be almost completely obscured by her hair and ears.

Surgical Procedure: an incision was made in Princess Margaret's temple running downward and backward to the apex of her ear. From here a crease ran toward her lobule in front of the ear, and the incision followed this crease around the lower margin of the lobule to a point slightly above the level of the tragus. From there, at an obtuse angle, it was carried backward and downward within the hairy margin of the scalp.

The edges of the incision were then undermined. First with a knife and then with a pair of scissors, the Princess's skin was lifted forward to the line of her jaw. The subcutaneous fatty tissue was scraped away with the knife. Large portions of connective tissue cling to the creases formed by frown lines, and some elements of these were retained in order to preserve the facial personality of the Princess. At two places the skin was pegged down firmly. The first was to the scalp at the top of her ear, the second was behind the ear to the scalp over the mastoid process. The first step was to put a strong suture in the correct position between the cheek flap anterior to the first point, and a second strong suture to the neck flap behind the ear. The redundant tissue was then cut away and the skin overlap removed with a pair of scissors.

At this point the ear was moved forward toward the chin, and the wound was then closed with interrupted sutures. It did not matter how strong the stitches were behind the ears because that part of the Princess's scarline was invisible in normal conditions.

Complications: haematoma formation is a dangerous sequela of this operation, and careful drainage with polythene tubing was carried out. In spite of these precautions blood still collected, but this blood was evacuated within 48 hours of the operation. It was not allowed to organize. In the early stages the skin around the area that had been undermined was insensitive, and it was not difficult to milk any collection of fluid backward to the point of drainage.

Scarring was hypertrophic at the points where tension was greatest: that is, in the temple and the region behind the ear, but fortunately these were covered by the Princess's hair. The small fine sutures which were not responsible for tension were removed at 4 days, and the strong sutures removed at the tenth day. The patient was then allowed to have a shampoo to remove the blood from her hair. All scarlines are expected to fade, and by the end of three weeks the patient was back in social circulation.

At a subsequent operation after this successful face lift, Princess Margaret's forehead wrinkles were removed. An incision was placed in the hairline and the skin lifted forward and upward from the temporal bone. The skin was then undermined and the excess tissue removed. The immediate result was good, but as a result of normal forehead movements relapse may occur unduly early after the operation. To remove the central frown line, the superciliary muscle was paralysed by cutting the branches of the seventh nerve passing centrally to it. A small knife-blade was inserted from the upper eyelid upward for 3 cm and then pressed down to the bone. External scars on the forehead often persist, and even in the best hands results are not always reliable. It was explained to Princess Margaret where the scars would lie, and the object of the intervention.

*Princess Margaret's Face Lift.*

The relationship between the famous and the public who sustain them is governed by a striking paradox. Infinitely remote, the great stars of politics, film and entertainment move across an electric terrain of limousines, bodyguards and private helicopters. At the same time, the zoom lens and the interview camera bring them so near to us that we know their faces and their smallest gestures more intimately than those of our friends.

Somewhere in this paradoxical space our imaginations are free to

179

range, and we find ourselves experimenting like impresarios with all the possibilities that these magnified figures seem to offer us. How did Garbo brush her teeth, shave her armpits, probe a worry-line? The most intimate details of their lives seem to lie beyond an already open bathroom door that our imaginations can easily push aside. Caught in the glare of our relentless fascination, they can do nothing to stop us exploring every blocked pore and hesitant glance, imagining ourselves their lovers and confidantes. In our minds we can assign them any roles we choose, submit them to any passion or humiliation. And as they age, we can remodel their features to sustain our deathless dream of them.

In a TV interview a few years ago, the wife of a famous Beverly Hills plastic surgeon revealed that throughout their marriage her husband had continually re-styled her face and body, pointing a breast here, tucking in a nostril there. She seemed supremely confident of her attractions. But as she said: 'He will never leave me, because he can always change me.'

Something of the same anatomizing fascination can be seen in the present pieces, which also show, I hope, the reductive drive of the scientific text as it moves on its collision course with the most obsessive pornography. What seems so strange is that these neutral accounts of operating procedures taken from a textbook of plastic surgery can be radically transformed by the simple substitution of the anonymous 'patient' with the name of a public figure, as if the literature and conduct of science constitute a vast dormant pornography waiting to be woken by the magic of fame.

# MAE WEST'S REDUCTION MAMMOPLASTY

The reduction in size of Mae West's breasts presented a surgical challenge of some magnitude, considerably complicated by the patient's demand that her nipples be retained as oral mounts during sexual intercourse. There were many other factors to be taken into account: Miss West's age, the type of enlargement, whether the condition was one of pure hypertrophy, the degree of ptosis present, the actual scale of enlargement and, finally, the presence of any pathology in the breast tissue itself. An outstanding feature of the patient's breasts was their obesity and an enlargement far beyond the normal. After the age of 50 years breast tissue may behave in a very unfortunate manner if the blood supply is in any way impaired. In the case of Miss West, therefore, it was decided that a pedical operation should be avoided and subtotal amputation with transposition of the nipples as free grafts was adopted as the procedure of choice.

In dealing with very large breasts in older subjects, it may be necessary to reduce the huge volume of breast tissue in two stages, since the radical reduction in one stage may well interfere with the nerve supply of the nipple and prevent the erection of the nipple during subsequent sexual excitation. Miss West was warned, therefore, of the possible need for a second operation.

## Procedure

A marked degree of asymmetry between Miss Mae West's two breasts was found. The left breast was appreciably larger than the right. The most important step before operating on the breasts was to ascertain carefully the sites proposed for the new nipples. Measurements were made in her suite before operation with Miss West sitting up. The mid-clavicular point was marked with Bonney's blue. Then, steadying each of the breasts in turn with both hands, the assistant drew a line directly down from this point to the nipple itself. The new nipple should fall on this line 7½ inches from the suprasternal notch. This corresponded to a position just below the midpoint of the upper arm when it was held close to the patient's chest. The entire skin of Miss West's chest wall was cleaned with soap and water and spirit, and then wrapped in sterile towels. Miss West was then ready for operation.

Removal of breast tissue. It was first considered how much breast tissue could be removed without damaging the blood supply to the nipple. The breast was brought forward and laid on a board of wood. A large breast knife was carried down from above, curving very close to the nipple. The final amount of tissue was not removed in the first stage, and the remaining tissue of the breast was folded round and up to judge whether the breast formed a shape that would be acceptable to Miss West, or whether it would be possible to remove more tissue.

Once more the entire field was reviewed for bleeding points. These were controlled by diathermy, but the pectoral vessels running down the border of pectoralis major were ligated. The skin covering was arranged to fit snugly over the newly formed breast. A curved intestinal clamp was used, but the fact that it fitted tightly on the skin margins did not appear to damage the vitality of the skin edges in any way.

All the stages described above were performed on the other side. It remained merely to bring out the nipples through new holes at the chosen position above the vertical suture line. Having found where the nipple would lie most comfortably, a circle of skin was excised. The nipple was then sutured very carefully into this circle.

The completion of the operation was to ensure that there were no collections of blood in the breast, and that the breast was adequately drained on both sides. Corrugated rubber drains running both vertically and horizontally were satisfactory. The breasts were very firmly bandaged to the chest wall using a many-tailed bandage. Firm pressure was applied to the lower half of the breast with Miss West lying absolutely flat on her back.

Post-operative recovery. The operation was a lengthy one and Miss West suffered a serious degree of surgical shock. Intravenous saline solution was given during the operation. The foot end of Miss West's bed was raised on blocks, and she was allowed to lie comfortably on her back until she recovered a normal pulse rate and a normal blood pressure.

Miss West was not allowed to go home before the fitting of an adequate supporting brassiere. It had a good deep section around the thorax, and the cups were of adequate size and gave good support from below. It was some time before Miss West's breasts reached their final proportions and shape, and there was no urgency about trimming scar lines until six months had passed. The left breast was then found to be too full in the lower quadrant, and the scar lines were unsatisfactory. Both these points were attended

**to. The ultimate results of this operation with regard to sexual function are not known.**

*Mae West's Reduction Mammoplasty.*

Still fondly remembered, Mae West was one of Hollywood's most effective safety valves, blowing a loud raspberry whenever the pressures of film industry self-inflation grew too great. No one in her admiring audience was ever in any doubt about the true purpose of that splendid body. Yet despite her earthiness, she retained a special magic of her own, and ended her days as a pop icon who might have been created by Andy Warhol. That he never decided to re-invent her reflects the fact, I think, that she got there before him, and might have dangerously subverted the whole Warhol ethos. Besides, Warhol was always at his best with vulnerable women.

Were her breasts too large? No, as far as one can tell, but they loomed across the horizons of popular consciousness along with those of Marilyn Monroe and Jayne Mansfield. Beyond our physical touch, the breasts of these screen actresses incite our imaginations to explore and reshape them. The bodies of these extraordinary women form a kit of spare parts, a set of mental mannequins that resemble Bellmer's obscene dolls. As they tease us, so we begin to dismantle them, removing sections of a smile, a leg stance, an enticing cleavage. The parts are interchangeable, like the operations we imagine performing on these untouchable women, as endlessly variable as the colours silkscreened on to the faces of Warhol's Liz and Marilyn.

**P.S.**

Ideas,
interviews
& features ...

# The Smile
*by J.G. Ballard*

Now that a nightmare logic has run its course, it is hard to believe that my friends and I thought it the most innocent caprice when I first brought Serena Cockayne to live with me in my Chelsea house. Two subjects have always fascinated me – woman and the bizarre – and Serena combined them both, though not in any crude or perverse sense. During the extended dinner parties that carried us through our first summer together three years ago her presence beside me, beautiful, silent and forever reassuring in its strange way, was surrounded by all kinds of complex and charming ironies.

No one who met Serena failed to be delighted by her. She would sit demurely in her gilt chair by the sitting-room door, the blue folds of her brocade gown embracing her like a gentle and devoted sea. At dinner, when my guests had taken their seats, they would watch with amused and tolerant affection as I carried Serena to her place at the opposite end of the table. Her faint smile, the most delicate bloom of that peerless skin, presided over our elaborate evenings with unvarying calm. When the last of my guests had gone, paying their respects to Serena as she watched them from the hall, head inclined to one side in that characteristic pose of hers, I would carry her happily to my bedroom.

Of course Serena never took part in any of our conversations, and no doubt this was a vital element of her appeal. My friends and I belonged to that generation of men who had been forced in early middle age, by sexual necessity if nothing else, to a weary acceptance of militant feminism, and there was something about Serena's passive beauty, her immaculate but old-fashioned make-up, and above all her unbroken silence that spelled out a deep and pleasing deference to our wounded masculinity. In all senses, Serena was the kind of woman that men invent.

But this was before I realized the true nature of Serena's character, and the more ambiguous role she was to play in my life, from which I wait now with so much longing to be freed.

Appropriately enough – though the irony then escaped me completely – I first saw Serena Cockayne at the World's End, in that area at the lower end of the King's Road now occupied by a cluster of high-rise apartment blocks but which only three years ago was still an enclave of second-rate antique shops, scruffy boutiques and nineteenth-century terrace housing over-ripe for redevelopment. Pausing on my way home from the office by a small curio shop announcing its closing-down sale, I peered through the sulphur-stained windows at the few remnants on display. Almost everything had gone, except for a clutch of ragged Victorian umbrellas collapsed in the corner like a decaying witch and an ancient set of stuffed elephants' feet. These dozen or so dusty monoliths had a special poignancy, all that remained of some solitary herd slaughtered for its ivory a century earlier. I visualized them displayed secretly around my sitting room, filling the air with their invisible but dignified presences.

Inside the shop a young woman attendant sat behind a marquetry desk, watching me with her head tilted to one side as if calculating in a patient way how serious a customer I might be. This unprofessional pose, and her total lack of response as I entered the shop, ought to have warned me off, but already I had been struck by the young woman's unusual appearance.

What I first noticed, transforming the dingy interior of the shop, was the magnificence of her brocaded gown, far beyond the means of a sales girl at this dowdy end of the King's Road. Against a lustrous blue field, a cerulean of almost Pacific deepness, the gold and silver patterning rose from the floor at her feet, so rich that I almost expected the gown to surge up and engulf her. By comparison, her demure head and shoulders, white bust discreetly revealed by the low bodice, emerged with an extraordinary serenity from this resplendent sea, like those of a domestic Aphrodite seated calmly astride Poseidon. Although she was barely beyond her teens, her hair had been dressed in a deliberately unfashionable style, as if lovingly assembled by an elderly devotee of twenties' film magazines. Within this blonde helmet her features had been rouged and powdered with the same lavish care, eyebrows plucked and hairline raised, without any sense of pastiche or mock nostalgia, perhaps by an eccentric mother still dreaming of Valentino.

Her small hands rested on her lap, apparently clasped together but in fact separated by a narrow interval, a stylized pose that suggested she was trying to hold to her some moment of time that might otherwise slip away. On her mouth hung a faint smile, at once pensive and reassuring, as if she had resigned herself in the most adult way to the vanishing world of this moribund curio shop.

'I'm sorry to see you're closing down,' I remarked to her. 'That set of elephants' feet in the window . . . there's something rather touching about them.'

She made no reply. Her hands remained clasped their millimetres apart, and her eyes stared in their trance-like way at the door I had closed behind me. She was sitting on a peculiarly designed chair, a three-legged contraption of varnished teak that was part stand and part artist's easel.

Realizing that it was some sort of surgical device and that she was probably a cripple – hence the elaborate make-up and frozen posture – I bent down to speak to her again.

Then I saw the brass plaque fastened to the apex of the teak tripod on which she sat.

SERENA COCKAYNE

Attached to the plaque was a dusty price ticket. '£250'.

In retrospect, it is curious that it took me so long to realize that I was looking, not at a real young woman, but at an elaborate mannequin, a masterpiece of the doll-maker's art produced by a remarkable virtuoso. This at last made sense of her Edwardian gown and antique wig, the twenties' cosmetics and facial expression. None the less, the resemblance to a real woman was uncanny. The slightly bowed contours of the shoulders, the too-pearly and unblemished skin, the few strands of hair at the nape of the neck that had escaped the wig-maker's attentions, the uncanny delicacy with which the nostrils, ears and lips had been modelled – almost by an act of sexual love – together these represented a *tour de force* so breathtaking that it all but concealed the subtle wit of the whole enterprise. Already I was thinking of the impact this life-size replica of themselves would have on the wives of my friends when I first introduced them to it.

A curtain behind me was drawn back. The owner of the shop, an adroit young homosexual, came forward with a white cat in his arms, chin raised at the sound of my delighted laughter. Already I had taken out my chequebook and had scribbled my signature with a flourish befitting the occasion.

\* \* \*

So I carried Serena Cockayne to a taxi and brought her home to live with me. Looking back at that first summer we spent together I remember it as a time of perpetual good humour, in which almost every aspect of my life was enriched by Serena's presence. Decorous and unobtrusive, she touched everything around me with the most delicious ironies. Sitting quietly by the fireplace in my study as I read, presiding like the mistress of the house over the dining table, her placid smile and serene gaze illuminated the air.

Not one of my friends failed to be taken in by the illusion, and all complimented me on bringing off such a coup. Their wives, of course, regarded Serena with suspicion, and clearly considered her to be part of some adolescent or sexist prank. However, I kept a straight face, and within a few months her presence in my house was taken for granted by all of us.

Indeed, by the autumn she was so much a part of my life that I often failed to notice her at all. Soon after her arrival I had discarded the heavy teak stand and substituted a small gilt chair on which I could carry her comfortably from room to room. Serena was remarkably light. Her inventor – this unknown genius of the doll-maker's art – had clearly inserted a substantial armature, for her posture, like her expression, never changed. Nowhere was there any indication of her date or place of manufacture, but from the scuffed patent-leather shoes that sometimes protruded below the brocade gown I guessed that she had been assembled some twenty years earlier, possibly as an actress's double during the great days of the post-war film industry. By the time I returned to the shop to inquire about her previous owners the entire World's End had been reduced to rubble.

One Sunday evening in November I learned rather more about Serena Cockayne. After working all afternoon in the study I looked up from my desk to see her sitting in the corner with her back to me. Distracted by a professional problem, I had left her there after lunch without thinking, and there was something rather melancholy about her rounded shoulders and inclined head, almost as if she had fallen from favour.

As I turned her towards me I noticed a small blemish on her left shoulder, perhaps a fleck of plaster from the ceiling. I tried to brush it away, but the discoloration remained. It occurred to me that the synthetic skin, probably made from some early experimental plastic, might have

5

begun to deteriorate. Switching on a table-lamp, I examined Serena's shoulders more carefully.

Seen against the dark background of the study, the down-like nimbus that covered Serena's skin confirmed all my admiration of her maker's genius. Here and there a barely detectable unevenness, the thinnest mottling to suggest a surface capillary, rooted the illusion in the firmest realism. I had always assumed that this masterpiece of imitation flesh extended no more than two inches or so below the shoulder line of the gown, and that the rest of Serena's body consisted of wood and papier mâché.

Looking down at the angular planes of her shoulder blades, at the modest curvatures of her well-concealed breasts, I gave way to a sudden and wholly unprurient impulse. Standing behind her, I took the silver zip in my fingers and with a single movement lowered it to Serena's waist.

As I gazed at the unbroken expanse of white skin that extended to a pair of plump hips and the unmistakable hemispheres of her buttocks I realized that the manikin before me was that of a complete woman, and that its creator had lavished as much skill and art on those never-to-be-seen portions of her anatomy as on the visible ones.

The zip had stuck at the lower terminus of its oxidized track. There was something offensive about my struggling with the loosened dress of this half-naked woman. My fingers touched the skin in the small of her back, removing the dust that had accumulated over the years.

Running diagonally from spine to hip was the hairline of a substantial scar. I took it for granted that this marked an essential vent required in the construction of these models. But the rows of opposing stitch-marks were all too obvious. I stood up, and for a few moments watched this partly disrobed woman with her inclined head and clasped hands, gazing placidly at the fireplace.

Careful not to damage her, I loosened the bodice of the gown. The upper curvatures of her breasts appeared, indented by the shoulder straps. Then I saw, an inch above the still-concealed left nipple, a large black mole.

I zipped up the gown and straightened it gently on her shoulders. Kneeling on the carpet in front of her, I looked closely into Serena's face, seeing the faint fissures at the apex of her mouth, the minute veins in her cheek, a childhood scar below her chin. A curious sense of revulsion and excitement came over me, as if I had taken part in a cannibalistic activity.

I knew now that the person seated on her gilt chair was no mannequin but a once living woman, her peerless skin mounted and for ever preserved by a master, not of the doll-maker's, but of the taxidermist's art.

At that moment I fell deeply in love with Serena Cockayne.

During the next month my infatuation with Serena had all the intensity of which a middle-aged man is capable. I abandoned my office, leaving the staff to cope for themselves, and spent all my time with Serena, tending her like the most dutiful lover. At huge expense I had a complex air-conditioning system installed in my house, of a type only employed in art museums. In the past I had moved Serena from warm room to cool without a thought to her complexion, assuming it to be made of some insensitive plastic, but I now carefully regulated the temperature and humidity, determined to preserve her for ever. I rearranged the furniture throughout the house to avoid bruising her arms and shoulders as I carried her from floor to floor. In the mornings I would wake eagerly to find her at the foot of my bed, then seat her by me at the breakfast table. All day she stayed within my reach, smiling at me with an expression that almost convinced me she responded to my feelings.

My social life I gave up altogether, discontinuing my dinner parties and seeing few friends. One or two callers I admitted, but only to allay their suspicions. During our brief and meaningless conversations I would watch Serena across the sitting room with all the excitement that an illicit affair can produce.

Christmas we celebrated alone. Given Serena's youth – at times when I caught her gazing across the room after some stray thought she seemed little more than a child – I decided to decorate the house for her in the traditional style, with a spangled tree, holly, streamers and mistletoe. Gradually I transformed the rooms into a series of arbours, from which she presided over our festivities like the madonna of a procession of altar-pieces.

At midnight on Christmas Eve I placed her in the centre of the sitting room, and laid my presents at her feet. For a moment her hands seemed almost to touch, as if applauding my efforts. Bending below the mistletoe above her head, I brought my lips to within that same distance from hers that separated her hands.

To all this care and devotion Serena responded like a bride. Her slim face, once so naive with its tentative smile, relaxed into the contented pose of a fulfilled young wife. After the New Year I decided to bring us out into the world again, and held the first of a few small dinner parties. My friends were glad to see us in such good humour, accepting Serena as one of themselves. I returned to my office and worked happily through the day until I set off for home, where Serena would unfailingly wait for me with the warm regard of a proud and devoted wife.

While dressing for one of these dinner parties it occurred to me that Serena alone of us was unable to change her costume. Unhappily the first signs of an excess domesticity were beginning to show themselves in a slight casualness of her personal grooming. The once elaborate coiffure had become unsettled, and the stray blonde hairs all too obviously caught the light. In the same way the immaculate make-up of her face now showed the first signs of wear and tear.

Thinking it over, I decided to call on the service of a nearby hairdressing and beauty salon. When I telephoned them they agreed instantly to send a member of their staff to my house.

And here my troubles began. The one emotion of which I had never suspected myself, and which I had never before felt for any human being, coiled around my heart.

The young man who arrived, bringing with him a miniature pantechnicon of equipment, seemed harmless enough. Although with a swarthy and powerful physique, there was something effeminate about him, and there was clearly no danger in leaving him alone with Serena.

For all his self-assurance, he seemed surprised when I first introduced him to Serena, his suave 'Good morning, madam . . .' ending in a mumble. Shivering in the cool air, he gazed at her open-mouthed, clearly stunned by her beauty and calm repose. I left him to get on with it and spent the next hour working in my study, distracted now and then by a few bars from *The Barber of Seville* and *My Fair Lady* that sounded down the stairs. When he had finished I inspected his work, delighted to see that he had restored every breath of her first glory to Serena. The over-domesticated housewife had vanished, and in her place was the naive Aphrodite I had first seen in the curio shop six months earlier.

So pleased was I that I decided to call on the young man's services again, and his visits became a weekly event. Thanks to his attentions, and my own devotion to the temperature and humidity controls, Serena's complexion regained all its perfection. Even my guests commented on the remarkable bloom of her appearance. Deeply contented, I looked forward to the coming spring and the celebration of our first anniversary.

Six weeks later, while the young hairdresser was at work in Serena's sitting room upstairs, I happened to return to my bedroom to collect a book. I could clearly hear the young man's voice, at a low pitch as if communicating some private message. I glanced through the open door. He was kneeling in front of Serena, his back to me, cosmetic pallet in one hand and paint stick in the other, gesticulating with them in a playful and mock-comical manner. Illuminated by his handiwork, Serena gazed straight into his face, her freshly painted lips almost moist with anticipation. Unmistakably, the young man was murmuring a discreet and private endearment.

During the following days I felt that my head had been seized by some kind of vice. As I tried helplessly to master the pain of that first intense jealousy, I was forced to realize that the young man was Serena's age, and that she would always have more in common with him than with me. Superficially our life continued as before – we sat together in the study when I returned from the office, I would carry Serena into the sitting room when my friends called, and she would join us at the dining table – but I was aware that a formal note had entered our relationship. No more did Serena pass the night in my bedroom, and I noticed that for all her calm smile I no longer caught her eye as I used to.

Despite my mounting suspicions, the young hairdresser continued to make his calls. Whatever crisis through which Serena and I were passing, I was determined not to give in. During the long hour of his visits I had to fight through every second to prevent myself from rushing up the staircase. From the hall I could often hear his voice murmuring in that insinuating tone, louder now as if he were trying to incite me. When he left I could sense his contempt.

It would take me an hour before I could walk slowly up the stairs to Serena's room. Her extraordinary beauty, relit by the taper of the young man's flattery, made my anger all the greater. Unable to speak, I would pace around her like a doomed husband, aware of the subtle changes to Serena's face. Although in every way more youthful, reminding me painfully of the thirty years that separated us, her expression after each visit became fractionally less naive, like that of a young wife contemplating her first affair. A sophisticated wave now modulated the curve of blonde hair that crossed her right temple. Her lips were slimmer, her mouth stronger and more mature.

Inevitably I began an affair with another woman, the separated wife of a close friend, but I made certain that Serena knew nothing of this or of the other infidelities that followed during the next weeks. Also, pathetically, I began to drink, and in the afternoons would sit around drunkenly in my friends' empty apartments, holding long imaginary conversations with Serena in which I was both abject and aggressive. At home I began to play the dictatorial husband, leaving her all evening in her room upstairs and moodily refusing to talk to her at the dining table. All the while, through paralysed eyes I watched the young hairdresser come and go, an insolent suitor whistling as he sauntered up the stairs.

After the last of his visits came the weary denouement. I had spent the afternoon drinking alone in a deserted restaurant, watched by the patient staff. In the taxi home I had a sudden confused revelation about Serena and myself. I realized that our breakdown had been entirely my fault, that my jealousy of her harmless flirtation with the young man had magnified everything to absurd proportions.

Released from weeks of agony by this decision, I paid off the taxi at my door, let myself into the cool air of the house and rushed upstairs. Dishevelled but happy, I walked towards Serena as she sat quietly in the centre of her sitting room ready to embrace her and forgive us both.

Then I noticed that for all her immaculate make-up and extravagant hair her brocade gown hung strangely from her shoulders. The right strap exposed the whole of her collar-bone, and the bodice had slipped forward as if someone had been fumbling with her breast. Her smile still hovered on her lips, calling on me in the most kindly way to resign myself to the realities of adult life.

Angrily I stepped forward and slapped her face.

How I regret that senseless spasm. In the two years that have passed I have had ample time to reflect on the dangers of an over-hasty catharsis. Serena and I still live together, but all is over between us. She sits on her gilt chair by the sitting-room fireplace and joins me at the dining table when I entertain my friends. But the outward show of our relationship is nothing more than the dried husk from which the body of feeling has vanished.

At first, after that blow to her face, little seemed to change. I remember standing in that room upstairs with my bruised hand. I calmed myself, brushed the face powder from my knuckles and decided to review my life. From then on I stopped drinking and went to the office each day, devoting myself to my work.

For Serena, however, the incident marked the first stage in what proved to be a decisive transformation. Within a few days I realized that she had lost something of her bloom. Her face became drawn, her nose more protuberant. The corner of her mouth where I had struck her soon became puffy and took on a kind of ironic downward twist. In the absence of the young hairdresser – whom I had sacked within ten minutes of striking her – Serena's decline seemed to accelerate. The elaborate coiffure which the young man had foisted upon her soon became undone, the straggling hairs falling on her shoulders.

By the end of our second year together Serena Cockayne had aged a full decade. At times, looking at her hunched on her gilt chair in the still brilliant gown, I almost believed that she had set out to catch and overtake me as part of some complex scheme of revenge. Her posture had slumped, and her rounded shoulders gave her the premature stoop of an old woman. With her unfocused smile and straggling hair she often reminded me of a tired and middle-aged spinster. Her hands had at last come together, clasped in a protective and wistful way.

Recently a far more disquieting development has taken place. Three years after our first meeting Serena entered upon a radically new stage of deterioration. As a result of some inherent spinal weakness, perhaps associated with the operation whose scars cross the small of her back, Serena's posture has altered. In the past she leaned forward slightly, but three days ago I found that she had slumped back in her chair. She sits there now in a stiff and awkward way, surveying the world with a critical and unbalanced eye, like some dotty faded beauty. One eyelid has partly closed, and gives her ashen face an almost cadaverous look. Her hands have continued on their slow collision, and have begun to twist upon each other, rotating to produce a deformed parody of themselves that will soon become an obscene gesture.

Above all, it is her smile that terrifies me. The sight of it has unsettled my entire life, but I find it impossible to move my eyes from it. As her face has sagged, the smile has become wider and even more askew. Although it has taken two years to achieve its full effect, that blow to her mouth has turned it into a reproachful grimace. There is something knowing and implacable about Serena's smile. As I look at it now across the study it seems to contain a complete understanding of my character, a judgment unknown to me from which I can never escape.

Each day the smile creeps a little further across her face. Its progress is erratic, revealing aspects of her contempt for me that leave me numb and speechless. It is cold here, as the low temperature helps to preserve Serena. By turning on the heating system I could probably dispose of her in a few weeks, but this I can never do. That smirk of hers alone prevents me. Besides, I am completely bound to Serena.

Fortunately, Serena is now ageing faster than I am. Helplessly watching her smile, my overcoat around my shoulders, I wait for her to die and set me free.                                                               **1976** ■

# An Investigative Spirit

*Travis Elborough talks to J.G. Ballard*

IN SEVERAL OF **your novels you have used a small community, the residents of a luxury housing development or a high-rise block for example, as a microcosm with which to explore the fragility of civil society. Do you think that your preoccupation with social regression, de-evolution even, stems from your childhood experiences in the internment camp when you saw, first hand, how easily the veneer of civilization could slip away?**

Yes, I think it does; although anyone who has experienced a war first hand knows that it completely overturns every conventional idea of what makes up day-to-day reality. You never feel quite the same again. It's like walking away from a plane crash; the world changes for you for ever. The experience of spending nearly three years in a camp, especially as an early teenage boy, taking a keen interest in the behaviour of adults around him, including his own parents, and seeing them stripped of all the garments of authority that protect adults generally in their dealings with children, to see them stripped of any kind of defence, often losing heart a bit, being humiliated and frightened – and we all felt the war was going to go on for ever and heaven knows what might happen in the final stages – all of that was a remarkable education. It was unique, and it gave me a tremendous insight into what makes up human behaviour.

**You've written that the landscape of even your first novel, *The Drowned World*, a ▶**

> 6 Anyone who has experienced a war first hand knows that it completely overturns every conventional idea of what makes up day-to-day reality. It's like walking away from a plane crash. 9

Author photograph by Jerry Bauer

## LIFE
## *at a Glance*

**BORN**
...............................
Shanghai, China, 1930

**EDUCATED**
...............................
Cathedral School,
Shanghai

The Leys School,
Cambridge

King's College,
Cambridge

**FAMILY**
...............................
Married Helen Mathews,
1956. One son, two
daughters

**LIVES**
...............................
Shepperton, Middlesex

## An Investigative Spirit *(continued)*

◄ **futuristic portrait of a flooded twenty-
first-century London, was clearly informed
by your memories of Shanghai. I wondered
if you could say a little about how, after
having possibly explored it obliquely in
your works of science fiction, you came to
write so directly about your childhood
experiences in *Empire of the Sun*?**

I had always planned to write about my
experiences of the Second World War,
Shanghai under the Japanese and the camp.
I knew that it was such an important event,
and not just for me. But when I came to
England in 1946 I had to face the huge
problem of adjusting to life here. England in
those days was a very, very strange place.
There was an elaborate class system that I'd
never come across in Shanghai. England . . .
it was a terribly shabby place, you know,
locked into the past and absolutely
exhausted by the war. It was only on a
technicality that we could be said to have
won the war; in many ways we'd lost it.
Financially we were desperate. I had to cope
with all this. By 1949 the Communists had
taken over China and I knew I would never
go back. So there seemed no point in
keeping those memories alive, I felt I had to
come to terms with life in England. This is,
after all, where I was educated. I got married
and began my career as a writer.

England interested me. It seemed to be a
sort of disaster area. It was a subject and a
disaster in its own right. I was interested in
change, which I could see was coming in a
big way, everything from supermarkets to jet
travel, television and the consumer society.

I remember thinking, my God, these things will bring change to England and reveal the strange psychology of these tormented people.

So I began writing science fiction, although most readers of science fiction did not consider me to be a science fiction writer. They saw me as an interloper, a sort of virus that had got into the cell of science fiction, entered its nucleus and destroyed it. But all this while I could see bits of my China past floating up and I knew I was going to write it up at some point.

**You studied medicine and have stated that you believe that the contemporary novelist should be like a scientist. Do you ever regret not qualifying as a doctor?**
I was very interested in medicine. The experience of dissecting cadavers for two years was a very important one for me, for all sorts of reasons. I do think that novelists should be like scientists, dissecting the cadaver . . . I would like to have become a doctor, but the urge to write was too great. I knew from friends of mine who were a year or two ahead of me that once you actually joined a London hospital or became a junior doctor the pressures of work were too great. I'd never have any time to write, and the urge to write was just too strong.

**Do you think there is a moral purpose to your fiction?**
I am not sure about that. I see myself more as a kind of investigator, a scout who is ▶

## An Investigative Spirit *(continued)*

◄ sent on ahead to see if the water is drinkable or not.

**As a scout or investigator you've been uncannily prescient, famously predicting Reagan's presidency in *The Atrocity Exhibition*, and I noticed that one commentator made reference to *The Drowned World* in the aftermath of the New Orleans disaster. Have you ever worried that you might be *too* prescient?** An investigator and a sort of early warning system, let's put it like that. I suppose one of the things I took from my wartime experiences was that reality was a stage set. The reality that you took for granted – the comfortable day-to-day life, school, the home where one lives, the familiar street and all the rest of it, the trips to the swimming pool and the cinema – was just a stage set. They could be dismantled overnight, which they literally were when the Japanese occupied Shanghai and turned our lives upside down. I think that experience left me with a very sceptical eye, which I've turned on to something even as settled as English suburbia where I now live. Nothing is as secure as we like to think it is. One doesn't just have to think of Hurricane Katrina and New Orleans – this applies to everything. A large part of my fiction tries to analyse what is going on around us, and whether we are much different people from the civilized human beings we imagine ourselves to be. I think it's true of all my fiction. I think that investigative spirit forms all my novels really. ■

# A Writing Life

**When do you write?**
Morning and early afternoon.

**Where do you write?**
In my sitting room.

**Why do you write?**
The great mystery.

**Pen or computer?**
Pen, then type myself.

**Silence or music?**
Silence.

**How do you start a book?**
I usually write a detailed synopsis.

**And finish?**
With a large full stop.

**Do you have any writing rituals or superstitions?**
No.

# Have You Read?

*A selection of J.G. Ballard's other books*

**The Complete Short Stories, Volumes I and II**

For over four decades, J.G. Ballard has been one of Britain's most celebrated novelists, but from the beginning he has been equally admired for his distinctive and highly influential short stories, the first of which – 'Prima Belladonna' and 'Escapement' – appeared in print in 1956. Arranged in order of publication and presented in two volumes, *The Complete Stories* provides an unprecedented opportunity to review the career of one of Britain's greatest writers.

**High-Rise**

Within the walls of an elegant forty-storey tower block, the affluent tenants are hell-bent on an orgy of destruction. Cocktail parties degenerate into marauding attacks on 'enemy' floors and the once-luxurious amenities become an arena for technological mayhem. In this classic visionary tale, human society slips into violent reverse as the inhabitants of the high-rise, driven by primal urges, recreate a world ruled by the laws of the jungle.

**The Day of Creation**

In parched Port-la-Nouvelle in central Africa Dr Mallory watches his clinic fail as constant warfare between a ragged band of guerrillas and the local chief of police causes the tribal residents to flee. In this drought-plagued and poverty-ridden country he dreams of discovering a third Nile to make the Sahara bloom. During his search an ancient tree stump is accidentally uprooted and water wells up, spreading until it becomes an enormous river. Naming it after himself, Mallory becomes obsessed with his creation, but almost as soon as he has discovered it he resolves to destroy it. With the once arid land now abounding in birds and beasts, he forges upriver in an old car ferry, clashing with hostile factions in a dangerous quest to find the source of his own creation.

### Cocaine Nights

When Charles Prentice arrives in Spain to investigate his brother's involvement in the death of five people in a fire in the upmarket coastal resort of Estrella de Mar, he gradually discovers that beneath the civilised, cultured surface of this exclusive enclave for Britain's retired rich there flourishes a secret world of crime, drugs and illicit sex. What starts as an engrossing mystery develops into a mesmerising novel of ideas: a dazzling work of the imagination from one of Britain's most original and controversial novelists.

### Super-Cannes

Paul Sinclair and his bright young wife Jane drive down to the south of France in his vintage Jaguar so that she can take up a post as doctor to the new community of Eden-Olympia, just above Cannes. According to its resident psychologist, Wilder Penrose, the community is 'a huge experiment in how to hothouse the future . . . an ideas laboratory ▶

### Have You Read? *(continued)*

◀ for the new millennium'. But Paul finds what he sees mystifying and unsettling, and when he learns that he and his wife have been housed in a villa whose previous occupant had been driven to massacre notable executives on a horrific shooting spree, he begins to look under the surface. For all the dawn-to-dusk hard work, for all its productivity and profits, Eden-Olympia is the venue for games of the most serious sort. So Paul joins in . . .

### *Millennium People*

When a bomb goes off at Heathrow it looks like just another random act of violence to psychologist David Markham. But then he discovers that his ex-wife Laura is among the victims. Acting on police suspicions, he starts to investigate London's fringe protest movements, falling in with a shadowy group based in the comfortable Thameside estate of Chelsea Marina. Led by a charismatic doctor, the group aims to rouse the docile middle classes to anger and violence, to free them from both the self-imposed burdens of civic responsibility and the trappings of a consumer society. Soon Markham is swept up in a campaign that spirals rapidly out of control. Every certainty in his life is questioned as the cornerstones of Middle England become targets and growing panic grips the capital.

### *Kingdom Come*

When the father of Richard Pearson, unemployed advertising executive and life-long rebel, is fatally wounded as a deranged mental patient opens fire on a crowd of shoppers at the Metro-Centre, Richard suspects that there is more to his father's death than meets the eye – especially when the main suspect is released without charge thanks to the dubious testimony of self-styled pillars of the community, including Julia Goodwin, the doctor who treated his father on his deathbed. Determined to unravel the mystery, Richard soon realises that the Metro-Centre, with its round-the-clock cable channel and sports clubs, lies at the very heart of his father's death. Consumerism rules the lives of everyone in the motorway towns and feeds the cravings of this bored community with its desperate need for something new, whatever the cost . . . ■

**If You Loved This,**
*You Might Like . . .*

***Mother London***
Michael Moorcock

***Naked Lunch***
William Burroughs

***1984***
George Orwell

***Fahrenheit 451***
Ray Bradbury

***A Clockwork Orange***
Anthony Burgess

***Brave New World***
Aldous Huxley

# Find Out More

SURF:

**www.jgballard.com**
A comprehensive website of all things Ballard, including links to interviews, reviews and much more.

**www.ballardian.com**
Alongside current and archival news about J.G. Ballard, this site hosts a forum for discussion of the author's work.

# J. G. BALLARD

# The Drowned World

'Britain's number one living novelist'

JOHN SUTHERLAND, *Sunday Times*

Fluctuations in solar radiation have caused the icecaps to melt and the seas to rise. Nature is on the rampage. London has been transformed into a primeval swamp, and within its submerged landscape giant lizards, dragonflies and insects compete for dominance. Human fertility is in decline and buildings sink beneath waters infested with decaying matter. Into this wasteland a group of intrepid scientists venture to record the flora and fauna of this new Triassic Age. Soon ghostly voices haunt their waking and nightmares permeate their sleep . . .

'One of the brightest stars in post-war fiction. This tale of strange and terrible adventure in a world of steaming jungles has an oppressive power reminiscent of Conrad'  KINGSLEY AMIS

'Powerful and beautifully clear . . . Ballard's potent symbols of beauty and dismay inundate the reader's mind'  BRIAN ALDISS

ISBN: 0-00-722183-5

# J. G. BALLARD

# Rushing to Paradise

'Pure Ballard. I read it with rapt fascination . . . wonderful'

WILLIAM BOYD

Veteran campaigner Dr Barbara Rafferty's obsessive crusade to save the albatross on the Pacific atoll of Saint-Esprit gains international support when millions of TV viewers witness the shooting of her young acolyte Neil Dempsey. Soon Dr Barbara turns the deserted island into a sanctuary – a remote paradise home for Neil, an odd team of eco-enthusiasts and a growing collection of the world's endangered species. As the extraordinary story unfolds it soon becomes clear that some species are more in danger than others . . .

'Ballard is a magician of the contemporary scene and a literary saboteur. *Rushing to Paradise* is a Wellsian drama of extremity and isolation . . . a parable about the ratlike behaviour of marooned human beings. No one else writes with such enchanted clarity or strange power'                                                                     *Guardian*

'A subversive version of *Lord of the Flies* . . . Ballard's relentless intelligence and wildly irreverent, absurdist humour collaborate in creating comically satiric sequences. A body blow to the pretensions of our century'                                                              *Irish Times*

'A satisfyingly bizarre mixture of fantasy and fact . . . a dystopian vision of a paradise island overrun by a band of environmentalists'                                                                                *Sunday Times*

'*Robinson Crusoe* in reverse. Teasing and sardonic . . . Ballard at his best'                                                              *Independent on Sunday*

ISBN: 0-00-654814-8

# J. G. BALLARD

# The Crystal World

'Something magical and not to be missed'                    *Guardian*

Through a 'leaking' of time, the west African jungle starts to crystal-lize. Trees metamorphose into enormous jewels. Crocodiles encased in second glittering skins lurch down the river. Pythons with huge blind gemstone eyes rear in heraldic poses. Most people flee the area in terror, afraid to face what they cannot understand. But some, dazzled and strangely entranced, remain to drift through this dreamworld forest: a doctor in pursuit of his ex-mistress, an enigmatic Jesuit wielding a crystal cross and a tribe of lepers search-ing for Paradise . . . In this tour de force of the imagination, the acclaimed author of *Crash*, *Empire of the Sun* and *Cocaine Nights* transports the reader into one of his most unforgettable landscapes.

'Beautifully rendered . . . Ballard the poet in full ecstatic blast'
ANTHONY BURGESS

'Brilliantly imagined . . . as a human adventure in a suddenly alien and frightening environment, the book is convincing and powerful'
*New Statesman*

'A haunting vision of diseased beauty . . . Ballard sustains it with extraordinary intensity'                    *Observer*

'Ballard transports us once more into his own mystical, glittering and poetic universe'                    *Sunday Telegraph*

ISBN: 0-586-02419-0

# J. G. BALLARD

# Empire of the Sun

'The best British novel about the Second World War'     *Guardian*

Based on J. G. Ballard's own childhood, *Empire of the Sun* is the extraordinary account of a boy's life in Japanese-occupied wartime Shanghai – a mesmerising and hypnotically compelling novel of war, of starvation and survival, of internment camps and death marches, which blends searing honesty with an almost hallucinatory vision of a world thrown utterly out of joint.

Shortlisted for the Booker Prize and the winner of both the *Guardian* Fiction Prize and the James Tait Black Memorial Prize, *Empire of the Sun* was later filmed by Steven Spielberg. Rooted as it is in the author's own disturbing experience of war in our time, it is one of a handful of novels by which the twentieth century will not only be remembered but judged.

'An incredible literary achievement and almost intolerably moving. A brilliant fusion of history, autobiography and imaginative speculation'     ANTHONY BURGESS

ISBN: 0-00-722152-5

# J. G. BALLARD

# The Kindness of Women

## The sequel to *Empire of the Sun*

'This is autobiography taken to the highest reaches of fiction, another wonderful novel of scorching power, shot with honesty and lyricism'                                                    *Observer*

'A dazzling construction, a sequence of chapters almost every one of which is a tour de force in its own right. He has put together the pieces of a fractured life here with honesty, humility and real brilliance'                                                                *Guardian*

'Possesses all the remarkable power and visceral impact of *Empire of the Sun*'                                                        *Daily Telegraph*

'With *The Kindness of Women* and its predecessor, Ballard has produced what is effectively the autobiography of sensibility. For my money, that sensibility is the most unusual and stimulating to have emerged in English literature since Graham Greene'
*Literary Review*

'Ballard is the most modern of writers; his art engages with the artefacts and obsessions of the second half of this century in a manner and with an intensity unmatched by any other writer. The book is full of mesmerising writing, classic examples of the Ballard style, paragraphs and pages that disturb and enthral. The blend is very potent and highly intoxicating'                    WILLIAM BOYD

'Brilliant . . . Ballard at his best'                        *Independent on Sunday*

ISBN: 0-00-654701-X